JOURNEY

JOURNEY

A SHORT STORY

VOLUME ①

MYKL WALSH

INKSHARES

This is a work of fiction. Names, characters, organizations, places, events, and incidents are either products of the author's imagination or are used fictitiously.

Copyright © 2015 Richard Saunders

All rights reserved.

No part of this book may be reproduced, or stored in a retrieval system, or transmitted in any form or by any means, electronic, mechanical, photocopying, recording, or otherwise, without express written permission of the publisher.

Published by Inkshares Inc., San Francisco, California
www.inkshares.com

Cover design by Marc J Cohen

ISBN: 9781941758472
eISBN: 9781941758489
Library of Congress Control Number: 2015939063

First edition

Printed in the United States of America

IN THE YEAR OF OUR LORD 10,001

The United States of Earth had been in power for over six thousand years. The federal government, working in close association with the private sector, had long since found cures for most of the world's most significant problems. People lived in near-utopian societies where they thrived for three to four hundred years on average. Most diseases were eradicated by the thirty-second century, the last war was fought in the forty-eighth, the aging process arrested in the seventy-fourth, and the rest, as they used to say, is history.

Meanwhile, on a godforsaken planet, within a parallel universe . . .
They landed at night.

The third planet from the sun had waited a very long time for this moment. Shuttle commander Simon Blackmon anxiously anticipated the touchdown. He has spent an eternity in suspended animation so that he could be the first. Simon had dreamed about this day since he was a child, and in a matter of minutes he would realize his destiny. To make first contact with intelligent beings from another world is an event of incomprehensible magnitude.

Simon's emotional level was so high—he could hardly contain himself. The doctor on the mother ship had given him a med designed to suppress emotion and promote rational response, but Simon had no intention of taking it.

With his face pressed tightly against the viewport, he nervously cracked to his first mate, "Todd, I don't see any reception party waiting on us."

"Ain't likely to either, if we can believe what the scanners upstairs are telling us," Todd flatly replied.

Simon and Todd Fischer had been resurrected only three months ago, following a two-thousand-year-long journey. The discovery of the positron field, coupled with advancements in quantum phase-skip methodologies, antimatter propulsion, and gravity revulsion had recently made long-distance space travel possible. These two best friends had been with the program since they were fourteen.

They'd awoken to both good and bad news. The good news was that the flight had gone well and they were all alive and on course. Using gravity-wave transmission fraqulles—a formatted unit of data carried within multiplexed frequency spectrums—they were able to communicate with their base while experiencing only half of the anticipated 128-hour time delay between sending and receiving transpackets. Still, they were not prepared for much of the news from "home."

Simon's wife was supposed to have undergone cryogenic suspension in the year following the departure of his flight. He learned that she had changed her mind and divorced him instead. She'd married another astronaut and had lived for eighty-seven more years before perishing in a meteor storm. Todd's wife and two children had died when their stasis unit failed because of improper monitoring and maintenance.

If they ever made it back, there would be no familiar faces to greet them. In fact, much of what they'd learned about their home planet was unfamiliar to them. Shaken from the revelations, they tried to focus on the job at hand, which was to explore the planet in this solar system that had, at least at one time, harbored intelligent life.

Several hundred years before their mission departed, a space drone had captured an intergalactic probe of alien origin. It was the first credible proof that intelligent beings existed elsewhere in the univial. The civilization that had designed and launched the probe was a primitive one, for sure, but, amazingly, they appeared to be human. The aliens who had launched the probe had supplied a mountain of data on how they lived, along with a map that showed where they were located, which was just next door in an adjacent universe. Simon and his crew had been dispatched to explore the planet while offering friendship and technology to its inhabitants.

From space, the planet appeared to be a cold, dry, and barren cinder. No life-forms could be detected, and background dispersion levels indicated that this small celestial orb had suffered from extreme radiation poisoning several thousand years ago, before it was wiped out. It appeared to have been victimized by nature's most violent weapon, a gamma-ray burster. Whatever calamity had befallen the planet had stripped it of its atmosphere and obliterated most of the surface features and structures that the once thriving civilization had created. The initial excitement and expectation of meeting the inhabitants of this world was subdued, and the mission was now classified as archeological instead of diplomatic.

Simon and Todd landed their shuttle in a region that showed signs of landscape intervention. The area had massive deposits of granite, and in several places it appeared that large sections had been carved out of the rock through an unnatural process. Simon conjectured that these cutouts were likely to have been fashioned by civilized beings in order to facilitate land-based travel.

After a soft touchdown Simon energized the protective force field while Todd ran through a checklist. Satisfied that they were secure, they bedded down for the night with the expectation of a grueling stay spent excavating the desolate landscape.

They arose at dawn and three hours later were ready to begin their quest to obtain evidence of the life-forms that had once flourished on this planet. Simon, his partner, and their respective acrobots mapped out then marked the perimeter of the dig and proceeded to scan the site. They monitored the results while skimming the ground with Subsurface Acoustical Wave (SAW) devices. These sophisticated scanners employed an old algorithm to discriminate between what was ordinarily found in nature from that which was manufactured or created by natural beings. The algorithm was based on the geometric precision principle first articulated by Archimendes of the ancient tribe of Thesonia, which states that only intelligent beings create structures that have a very high degree of perfection to them, i.e. perfect squares, rectangles, etc. Geometric precision rarely occurs in scale within a natural environment devoid of intervention from advanced species.

On the second day of the search, Simon registered a hit with his machine, which indicated that three rectangular-shaped objects were buried under eight feet of bituminous soil and rock. The two space- and time-traveling explorers rolled out the vaporizing excavator and positioned it over the freshly marked spot.

Simon set the machine for a depth of three inches above the first target while Todd and his acrobot left to retrieve an electrodynamic hoist. Once the setup was complete and properly aligned, Todd energized the vaporizer. A thin curtain of high-intensity laser light worked its way across a four-by-six-foot area, quickly reducing the surface matter to an elementary isotopic dust that was automatically vacuumed away. With each pass, two inches or so of terra firma would disappear. After a few minutes the machine reached a set point just above the target object and reverted to manual mode. Simon slowly and carefully excavated the remaining few inches until the top of the object became visible. Next he ran a tight beam around the periphery of the article, readying it for extraction. The pair then removed the vaporizer unit and positioned a magnomic retriever over the crypt-like opening. Tractor beams grabbed the object and gently rocked it from side to side, freeing the bottom.

Todd switched to retraction mode and brought the buried treasure to the surface. The lone inhabitants of this world could now examine their find. The item was wrapped in several layers of ultrasonically sealed Mylar sheets. It measured three and a half hands by two and a half hands with a depth of two lmrs. It weighed fifty-seven kronrs. Constructed of plastic alloys, its skin was two gry thick. The lid was hermetically and ultrasonically welded, and the seal had not been penetrated. Swedvig readings indicated that the interior was stabilized with reverse pressurization in a class-three vacuum state. Two more identical containers were removed from lower depths in the same vault.

"Whatever's inside these tubs, someone took extreme care to ensure that they would survive for a very long time," Todd quipped. All business as usual, Simon directed his acrobot to place the containers in the ship's cargo hold. "We're just getting started, Todd, I have no time for contemplation right now. We've got eighty-seven parsxs of this planet to investigate, and we're going to cover every notch of it."

For whatever reasons, Simon would not admit that he was every bit as curious as to the contents of this find as was his friend.

After spending two more weeks collecting samples and recording scientific data, the shuttle and its crew returned to the mother ship with its cargo bay filled to capacity. An engineer in the larger vessel immediately informed Simon of an interesting discovery.

While orbiting the planet, conducting experiments, and analyzing data, the chief engineer had noted several similarities between this planet and their own. The most significant and striking correlation related to a freak accident that happened in the early stages of the planet's formation. Some four and a half billion years ago, while the outer crust of the globe was still being formed through the cooling of the surface layer, a large and very special heavenly object had crashed into the planet, penetrating the crust and eventually coming to rest in the center of the celestial body. Although the intruder was made up of numerous substances, it was primarily metal, mostly iron. Cruising close by the sun, then picking up additional heat through atmospheric friction, it was a molten, liquefied ball at the time of the immense collision.

The force of the impact was so great that it knocked the planet into a new and more favorable orbital path. The massive amount of debris that was thrown into space eventually coalesced to form the planet's moon. Once the metallic meteor stopped oscillating, it eventually settled into the center of its new host. This liquid ball of iron, rotating out of phase in relation to the planet's crust, created a magnificently powerful magnetic field. This field was crucial to the planet's ability to nurture and support the evolutionary processes that are the key to the development of advanced lifeforms. Although microbiological creatures are relatively abundant throughout the univial, they rarely evolve to advanced levels of intelligent life. Simon and Todd's home planet also shared this same anomaly. These two otherwise insignificant tiny orbs both owe their fortunes to a coincidental, seemingly random cataclysmic cosmological event. Alone among their peers, they won the mother of all lotteries.

The crew began to prepare for the long ride home. Doc checked out the suspended-animation chambers, and one by one the staff was carefully cycled into the long-term preservation state. After everyone else had been suspended, Simon was alone, save for the acrobot, who would eventually suspend him before shutting herself down.

The commander would have to wait a few months before he could be preserved, however. He needed to remain animated in order to help guide the ship out of occupied space and safely to the intergalactic void before energizing the antimatter drives that would warp the craft into twilight speed under automatic pilot.

. . .

Simon dragged the plastic storage tub out of the interior cargo bay and contemplated opening it. He had been given a directive from his controller on Earth to leave it sealed, but his loyalties were not the same as when he'd left home all those interminable years ago. He was anxious, lonely, and felt completely disconnected from his origins. He worried about not being able to adjust to a society that felt so alien to him. He scanned the parcel again to make sure that nothing inside posed any biohazards or threats to the spacecraft. I really shouldn't open it, he reasoned. No sense starting out on the wrong leg with the regime back home."

Walking about the cabin, running through his checklist, Simon's eyes kept wandering back to the vessel that he had neglected to return to storage. His curiosity taunted him, and without anyone else on board to tell him not to, he directed his acrobot to place the tub in an isolation chamber in the examination room. The chamber was drawn down into a class-three vacuum state while Simon energized a remote-controlled armbot, carefully cutting away the outer wrapping of the tub and exposing the sealed lip along the edge of the cover. A negative ultrasonic wide-angle beam quickly freed the cover of its bonds. The lid was then removed, exposing the contents. Peeling back a few sheets of moisture-absorbing material revealed two layers of Mylix shock-absorbing panels that lined the container. After lifting off these surface sheets, the armbot began to extract the various items contained within the ancient coffin. Every item had been vacuum-sealed in vellum. The armbot placed each piece on a shelf where it scanned them and sent the data to the computer to be categorized, with its original position in the container charted in three dimensions. The chamber was flooded with high-intensity UVW light to destroy any potentially hazardous microbes, then slowly pressurized, until it reached equilibrium. Finally, a molecular wind sweep sucked up any remaining loose particulates as fresh air was cycled in and out of the chamber until it was pure. Simon could now enter the clean room and examine his find.

He could tell almost immediately that it was some type of time capsule. He was familiar with the primary written and spoken languages of this planet, having learned through a brain dump of information gathered from the intercepted probe. Simon determined that he was in possession of a number of items that had once belonged to someone named Richard Saunders, who had lived on this planet during a period bridging the second and third millennium AD.

The artifacts, at first glance, seemed to represent samples of everyday items common to people who lived at the time and place of the internment. One inner container was found to possess a complete table setting for one along with a wine chalice. These items appeared to be substantially older than everything else in that container and were obviously considered to be highly valuable by the owner, considering the way that they were separated and packed.

Among the eclectic set of contents were several scientific papers nestled between other items apparently representative of the era in which they were interned. The papers were mostly standard physics stuff, detailing quantum mechanics, universal field superstring constructs, the grand universal theory, etc., things that any high school student back home would know. They were well preserved on specially treated acid-free paper. Each page had been ultrasonically encapsulated in Mylar sheaths. Simon picked up a book that had been prominently placed on top of everything else. He cut away the translucent protective covering, exposing the cover. It was a novel; a fiction detailing the lifetime adventures of one Lawrence R. Howard. The story was written by Saunders, and the setting paralleled his own time and space. Simon took the novel back to his crib and began to read.

Journey, A Short Story *is now suspended. It will continue when Simon finishes reading*

SecretAgentMan.

SECRETAGENTMAN

The Life & Times of Lawrence R. Howard

Volume I

1955–1960

Serialized Fiction from

Richard Saunders

DISCLAIMER

SecretAgentMan takes place on an Earthlike planet within a parallel universe.

Although inspired in part by actual events, the following story is fictional and does not depict any actual persons or events. Any similarity to actual persons, places, planets, or events is either purely coincidental or due to the inherent nature of closely aligned parallel universes.

	Albert Einstein	Lawrence Ronald Howard	Richard Saunders
IQ	Genius	Genius	Average on a good day
Year Born / Year Deceased	1879–1955	1956–_____	1956–_____
Astrological Sign	Pisces	Pisces	Pisces
Myers-Briggs Personality Type	INTP	INTP	INTP
Lived in	Eastern US	Eastern US	Eastern US
Height	5' 8"	5' 8"	5' 8"
Weight	170 lbs.	170 lbs.	170 lbs.

Of what is significant in one's own existence one is hardly aware, and it certainly should not bother the other fellow. What does a fish know about the water in which it swims all of his life?

The bitter and the sweet come from the outside, the hard from within, from one's own efforts. For the most part I do the thing which my own nature drives me to do. It is embarrassing to earn so much respect and love for it.

Arrows of hate have been shot at me too; but they never hit me, because somehow they belonged to another world, with which I have no connection whatsoever.

I live in that solitude which is painful in youth, but delicious in the years of maturity.

—Albert Einstein, "Self-Portrait," *Out of My Later Years*, 1935

SERIES CONTENTS

1955—Life Cycles
1956—A Second Son
1957—Duty Calls
1958—Weston Communications, Inc.
1959—A New Addition
1960—A Coup for Catholics

CHAPTERS IN FUTURE VOLUMES

1961—The Lost Generation
1962—First Grade
1963—The End of Camelot
1964—The Young Scientist
1965—The Professor
1966—The Magician
1967—It's a Girl
1968—A World Gone Mad
1969—From Earth to the Moon
1970—High School
1971—A Family of Nine
1972—Bloody Sunday
1973—Coeds!
1974—A Presidential Disgrace
1975—The Working Man
1976—The Martial Artist
1977—Friendship Renewed
1978—Only the Good Die Young
1979—Vatican Intrigue

1980—An Olympic Year
1981—A Friend in Need
1982—Dr. Demming, I Presume
1983—Saving Sight
1984—An Orwellian Year
1985—Suicide and Betrayal
1986—Triumph and Tragedy
1987—The Baton is Passed
1988—Something for Joey
1989—Lost Motivation
1990—UMass / Boston
1991—A Beautiful Day on Loon Mountain
1992—The Patriarch Departs
1993—A Streak of Luck
1994—Wild Bill
1995—Destiny
1996—A Split Personality
1997—Locust Emerges
1998—The Data Vault
1999—Apocalypse Now?
2000—Dawn in a New Age
2001—Satan Knocks on Our Door
2002—The Catholic Crisis
2003—Leonardo's Cipher
2004—I Wanna Be Elected
2007—The Trask Affair
To be continued . . . to 2015 and beyond

CONTENTS

A Star Is Born 21
Foreword 25
Ancient Times 29
Chronology of The Defender 30

VOLUME 1
    1955—Life Cycles 32
    1956—A Second Son 38
    1957—Duty Calls 46
    1958—Weston Communications, Inc. 50
    1959—A New Addition 53
    1960—A Coup for Catholics 56

PREVIEW OF FUTURE VOLUMES
    1994—Wild Bill 61
    1995—Destiny 79
    1996—A Split Personality 82
    1998—The Data Vault 91
    2003—Leonardo's Cipher 99
    2004—The Columbine Memorial 104
    2007—The Trask Affair 114
    2015—Aspirations 151

Acknowledgments 152
About the Author 154

A Star Is Born:

A Review of SecretAgentMan

SecretAgentMan was born in the restless mind of nine-year-old Richard Franklin Saunders in 1965. Rich spent much of that year living in a fantasy world occupied by heroic characters from television, literature, religion, movies, and comic books. Overwhelmed by creative impulses, young Saunders schemed to invent a superhero of his own, one who could compete with and defeat any foe, real or imagined.

In developing this project, Saunders decided that his protagonist's powers should be restricted to the abilities of a mortal man. Starting with a reincarnated Albert Einstein, Saunders added characteristics from John Drake, Harry Houdini, James Bond, and Fred Demara to his model. The first incarnation of *SecretAgentMan* on paper occurred in October 1965 and consisted of a single four-panel comic strip. This original strip has been preserved and today it lies in a secret underground storage vault located somewhere on public land in New Hampshire.

The moniker L. Ron Howard was first applied in 1968. The *L* represents Lawrence, the Massachusetts textile-mill town where both

Saunders and Demara spent their formative years.

Early on, Saunders was fascinated by the story of *The Great Impostor*. His family had a direct connection to this world-famous persona. Saunders's grandfather had rented an apartment in his multifamily house to the Demara family, and his grandmother often babysat the young impostor. When Saunders saw the film in 1967, he was surprised to find both his school and church prominently featured in this major Hollywood movie. Tony Curtis played the impostor and Karl Malden played the pastor of St. Augustine church. Rich was very impressed. He was also inspired. A week after seeing the movie, he checked the book out of the Lawrence Public Library.

The following paragraph was excerpted from *The Great Impostor* by Robert Crichton: (Random House, 1959).

> It can't be said that Lawrence produces impostors but it can be argued that if a person has some bent toward impostoring and the roots for it are there, they couldn't find a better place for them to seize hold and flourish. Such prosaic restraints on a boy's lively imagination as tradition and stability were almost totally lacking in Lawrence. The situation was fluid and there were people who drowned in it every day in Lawrence.

That was all the encouragement Saunders needed. He knew in that instant that he would dedicate himself to being an impostor and that Fred Demara was the standard by which he would measure his success. *Robert Crichton said that Lawrence, Massachusetts, was the best place in the world to learn how to become an impostor! How can a kid pass up a chance like that?* was Saunders's view. *All the other kids in the world who might want to become impostors don't have the advantage or the opportunity that I have!* Rich realized that it would be foolish to try to imitate some of Demara's more dangerous impersonations. For instance, he wasn't going to be performing surgery on anyone or putting people (other than himself) in danger with his impostor tactics. His goal was to become an amusing and entertaining impostor, not a dangerous or illegal one. In 1969, after seeing the movie *2001: A Space Odyssey*, thirteen-year-old Richard Franklin Saunders decided to wait until after he crossed the bridge to the magical new millennium before releasing the groundbreaking literary masterwork that had become his passionate hobby.

With varying levels of energy and enthusiasm, Saunders has worked alone and in complete secrecy, slowly and methodically evolving his characters and plotting the epic adventure that is about to unfold on these pages.

In what can only be described as an extraordinary accomplishment, Saunders has successfully acted out much of his script in numerous real-life situations while involving many others who had no idea what was really going on. Soon, people like Michael Dukas, Don Breen, Daniel Trask, Katie Parry, William Wilde, and countless others will know the truth behind their relationship with Mr. Saunders!

Saunders has emerged from the shadows as a huge talent, finally allowing the rest of us to enter his previously hidden world.

It is believed that this real-life journey of living, breathing, and nurturing this project, without ever betraying its secret, is an accomplishment that is unprecedented in the history of literature.

Please join me in congratulating Richard Saunders for this stunning literary achievement.

—Joshua Quincy

Note from Richard Saunders: My friend Josh here is obviously way over the top. Although I appreciate his efforts, I know better than to believe my own press. I would advise that my readers take a highly skeptical attitude regarding anything that comes out of the publicity and promotions departments. Don't believe any of it, unless someone proves to you that it is true. Just enjoy the fiction and assume that it is entirely fictional. Who cares if some of it might or might not come from real-life events? If the story fails to entertain, it isn't worth your time and it doesn't matter what may be true or not.

More nonsense will be found in the foreword from my good friend Mykl Walsh. I advise you to just skip over it, as some of what he says is repetitive or reflective of Quincy's well-meaning narrative.

FOREWORD

Richard Saunders has been a close friend of mine since 1971. It wasn't until almost thirty years later, however, that I first realized that I didn't really know him at all.

We were heading north on Interstate 93, returning home from a pleasant afternoon spent at Fenway Park in Boston. I was driving, and Rich was the only passenger left, having already dropped off Eddie and Paul in Stoneham. We were making the rounds of our customary and ritualized topics of conversation when Rich slipped seamlessly into a story about his childhood. What started out sounding like an innocent and amusing anecdotal snippet from his early youth gradually expanded into an elaborate and epic tale that nearly left me speechless. Boiled down to its essence, here is what I learned on that fateful Sunday in August.

In 1965 Rich decided to create a fictional superhero based on a loose compilation of character sets from the likes of Albert Einstein, Harry Houdini, Fred Demara, John Drake, and James Bond.

SecretAgentMan came to life as a four-panel comic strip that gradually evolved into a series of short stories, then a novel. Rich looked deep into the future and decided that his creation would not make its public debut until sometime after the dawn of the new millennium.

Apparently possessed with the patience of a saint, Rich made a list of subject areas and skills where his superhero would need to possess a high level of expertise. Here comes the extraordinary part. He then endeavored to develop that expertise within himself, in order to have the credibility he would need to make this super-character seem *real*.

From astronomy to computers and electronics to magic, martial arts, and Zen, the list was extensive, eventually containing over two-dozen entries. The idea that any one person could hope to reach a respectable level of expertise in so many disciplines would seem to be an impossibility to most of us. But not to nine-year-old Richard Saunders, who, as I am still learning, is decidedly not like the rest of us. Comforted that he had several decades to acquire this mother load of knowledge and skill, he began to attack his list with a vengeance. Proceeding methodically and steadfastly, he checked one item after another off the list. He spent months, sometimes years, concentrating almost exclusively on a particular topic or skill until he felt that he had reached the required level of mastery.

Honoring a self-imposed vow of silence, Rich has quietly been plotting his protagonist through a voyage in time that spans the second half of the twentieth century and bridges the next. In countless instances over these years he has taken the highly unusual step of acting out his plotlines in real life, in real time, while surreptitiously involving others (including myself) in his plots. His targets never had any idea what the game was really all about. Now we know. For a fiction that is so fantasy driven, the consistent entwinement with reality is a truly remarkable feat.

Rich defines his deliciously innovative approach to creating literature as "method writing." He has woven his tale so skillfully into real-life situations that I believe it is now nearly impossible to separate the facts from the fiction in the story, and I challenge anyone who reads this novel to try. The supernatural aspects are, of course, all fiction . . . I think.

I pulled my car into his driveway, my head spinning from the revelations that I am now privy to. Rich was not done surprising and astounding me, though. He invited me in to examine "some documents." He allowed me into his home office for the first time ever, and I had my mind scrambled even further. To my eyes the lair was a complete mess; to Rich it was home. Books, manuscripts, newspapers and clippings, files and folders, computers and electronic paraphernalia littered the room. Stuff was piled on top of tables and stacked under them. Rich would pick up a particular object and briefly explain what it was, then put it down in another spot. He reached into a two-foot-high stack of papers and effortlessly pulled out the page he was looking for. He was especially excited when he revealed the work that he had done for the Pentagon's Advanced Research Projects Agency (ARPA) unit, something that had served to solidify the bond with his late father more than anything else.

A few items were so precious that they deserved their own special storage space. A yellowed notebook from 1965 merited such treatment. It contained the first time that the *SecretAgentMan* concept was placed into print. Inside was the original list of skill sets, the first four-panel comic strip, and a synopsis. The raw material for this story is contained in thousands of pages of handwritten text, sorted by year. From this mountain of evidence, Saunders planned to produce his novel.

In what I believe to be a brilliant stroke of promotional genius, Saunders has sealed his "evidence" in three carefully prepared plastic containers, each the size of a footlocker. A few weeks ago we began burying these twentieth-century time capsules deep into the New Hampshire soil. The GPS location of this treasure will be hidden in code within the text of the first volume of *SecretAgentMan*.

What does one do when confronted with such a startling and impressive disclosure? If you're like me, you immediately begin to think of ways that you can horn in on and profit from the situation, even if it means taking advantage of your best friend!

Numb as Novocain, I was apparently clearheaded enough to ask if I could write the foreword to the novel. A few weeks later I called Rich and told him of an idea I had about a futuristic scientific expedition wherein astronauts descend upon a dead planet and unearth his long hidden treasure. Rich has never refused any favor that I've asked of him, and the rest, as they say, is history.

From this incredible background, *SecretAgentMan* was born. May God bless the spirit of L. Ron Howard, and may he live forever.

—Mykl Walsh

ANCIENT TIMES

In ancient times, forces of evil gathered from distant corners of the universe, united in their quest to achieve a common goal.

From this unholy alliance emerged a plan to launch a full-scale assault for control of the planet Earth.

God, in her infinite wisdom, anointed one spirit to lead the defense, sending The Chosen One on a journey of seemingly endless incarnations.

In each lifetime he will acquire a small portion of the strength and wisdom that he will need to repel the invading storm.

Some say there are signs the assault is near; whisperers claim that The Defender, an ordinary mortal, walks among us.

CHRONOLOGY OF THE DEFENDER

... Ptolemy	87–150
... da Vinci	1452–1519
Copernicus	1473–1543
Jöns Svinhufvud	1544–1564
Galileo Galilei	1564–1642
Isaac Newton	1642–1727
John De Hart	1728–1795
Nicolas Carnot	1796–1831
James Maxwell	1831–1879
Albert Einstein	1879–1955

February 1956: Ten months after the death of Albert Einstein, Lawrence Ronald Howard is born at Holy Family Hospital in Methuen, Massachusetts. An average-looking child, he gave no outward sign that behind innocent blue eyes, his mind burned with genius.

He would spend a lifetime walking a tightrope, blindly negotiating the dark, narrow corridor between brilliance and madness. Unaware that he is guided by forces unseen, Ron embarks on a strategy to hide his genius, to cloak it behind a facade of ordinariness.

To the outside world he was an everyman, a simple tradesman without an estate. In truth, he was a giant of his time. Using little more than the power of his own mind, he profoundly altered the scientific and political landscape of the twentieth and twenty-first centuries.

As the third millennium approached, his fiercest challenger beckoned. It is revealed to Ron that his spirit had been groomed to defend the planet against an all-out assault by the forces of evil. A reluctant warrior, he would emerge from the shadows to accept his fate and assume the role that he was born to fulfill.

At the dawn of a new era, one man stood in the way of Lucifer's greatest triumph.

1955

Life Cycles

A pril 18, Princeton Hospital, Princeton, New Jersey
The chalk on the blackboard of his mind was beginning to blur as Albert rested his head back on the pillow, eyes closed. "Of course!" he whispered in the dark, exhaling his last breath.

. . .

Mary Howard awoke suddenly and glanced at the bedside alarm clock. Her husband, Joe slept silently beside her. "Quarter past one," she read while slowly rising and making her way to the darkened kitchen to fix a hot cup of Lipton tea. Suddenly she felt dizzy, then faint. Leaning against the counter for support, she steadied herself. *God, I hope I'm not pregnant again,* she thought while slowly lowering herself into a chair. After a minute the spell had passed, leaving in its wake the uncomfortable feeling that something inside her had changed.

Now twenty-five years old, Mary had married at nineteen and already had been blessed with three children: Ann, aged four; John, three; and Patricia, six months old. This ordinary family of five lived in a government-subsidized housing project on Memorial Circle in Andover, Massachusetts. Similar complexes had been erected around the country to house the growing families of military veterans in the post–World War II baby boom era. Joe had served with the Army Air Corps at the tail end of the conflict and had finished his tour attached to an Army Intelligence unit stationed in Germany as part of the Allied Occupation Forces.

Struggling to support a young and growing family, Joe worked for his brother's laundry business in Andover center. Equipped with a GI Bill–enabled bachelor's degree in accounting from Merrimack College—a member of the school's first graduating class in 1951—Joe had yet to secure the level of employment that his education had promised.

IN OTHER SEMINAL EVENTS FROM 1955:

President Eisenhower sent a group of "advisors" to South Vietnam for the first time.

February 17: Tenley Albright from Newton, Massachusetts, won the World Figure Skating Championships in Vienna.

April 12: Dr. Jonas Salk announced that his team had successfully tested a polio vaccine. It was soon approved for widespread use.

May 27: Norm Zauchin had ten RBI's as the Boston Red Sox beat the Washington Senators 16–0.

November 5: Marty McFly arrived in Hill Valley, California. He returned to 1985 one week later.

December 1: Rosa Parks was arrested in Montgomery, Alabama, for refusing to give up her bus seat to a white man. This was the tiny spark that ignited the modern civil rights era for African Americans.

Joe with his platoon in Germany, 1944

Joe at Merrimack College's first graduation ceremony in Andover, Massachusetts, 1951

Mary Howard with her firstborn at Memorial Circle, Andover, Massachusetts, 1952

Ann, John, and Patricia

1956

A Second Son

January 11: In the maternity ward at Holy Family Hospital in Methuen, Massachusetts, Adrian Nelson arrived at just the right place and time to fulfill her destiny. Her spirit had been paired with The Defender eons ago. Unknowingly, these two soul mates traveled through space and time together. In every incarnation they would meet, seemingly for the first time.

. . .

"This baby is in no hurry," Mary told Dr. Shanley during her monthly checkup on February 12. Two weeks past due, there was no sign that labor would be commencing any time soon.

Being a child of destiny, he would, by necessity, be born under the sign of Pisces. Finally, on February 25, after an excruciatingly long and uncomfortable pregnancy, Mary delivered her second son at Holy Family Hospital.

. . .

At midnight, a bitterly cold wind tore through the crowd gathered around the tombstone of Marie de Blanchefort in the churchyard at Rennes-le-Château, France. A small group of men and women bowed, prayed, and performed ancient rituals before raising a toast in solemn tribute to the long anticipated birth of the one known only as The Defender.

A few weeks later this golden child was baptized into the Roman Catholic faith at St. Augustine church. Christened Lawrence Ronald Howard, he was named after the Immigrant City that had welcomed generations of poor and tired refugees who came to the United States in search of the American Dream. Howard's own ancestors had migrated to Lawrence from Ireland during the potato famine and had been instrumental members of the labor force that built the carefully planned industrial city. In 1912, the labor movement in the United States achieved one of their earliest and most significant victories in Lawrence, in what came to be known as the "Bread and Roses" strike.

The Howard baby was born with a severely swollen and misshapen head, though doctors assured the parents that this was a temporary condition and was no cause for alarm. By late March the swelling had subsided and his features became more defined. As the months passed, his individuality began to emerge.

Ron possessed a free and engaging smile, though his eyes were his most striking feature. They were a hypnotic blue-green mix with chameleon qualities. As he grew older, his natural good looks, combined with a light and pleasant personality, allowed him to make friends easily. His preference, though, would be to live a clandestine, semisolitary existence.

Belying outward appearances, all was not completely well with the child. Unknown to the family doctor or to his parents, Ron was born with a rare congenital birth defect. A seemingly random anomaly: a polygenic deviation located within a series of genes on chromosomes eighteen and twenty-one produced a condition known in layman's terms as a "racing brain." It is at once both a gift and a curse. Sometimes referred to as "the Genius Affliction," this particular syndrome has produced some of the brightest and most tragic minds that the world has known. While a racing brain can sometimes produce a brilliantly creative personality, it can also lead to depression, mania, schizophrenia, and other mental illnesses. Little did anyone suspect that behind those bright-blue eyes lay a mind that burned with genius.

Another consequence of this condition was that Ron was only able to sleep for three or four hours each night. The first three Howard children were sound sleepers. Mary was not so fortunate with her fourth offspring.

. . .

The most important event of the time was unknown to almost all but those in the heavens or in Hades. In June 1956, an organization called the Priory of Sion registered with the bureau of records in Annemasse, France. The document named four officers: Andre Bonhomme, president; Jean de Laval, vice-president; Pierre Plantard, secretary-general; and Armand Defago, treasurer. The Priory of Sion is an ultrasecret religious society with an unbroken history that dates back, under various names and guises, some two-thousand-plus years. Normally, they operated as a small group of highly influential people whose main function was to keep and closely guard the divine secrets and early Christian texts and artifacts that had been hidden away from the Vatican and passed down through twenty centuries. Only four persons in each generation were allowed to possess full knowledge of the secrets and their locations. The keepers worked together to devise a succession plan and a security plan to ensure that their secrets would survive their deaths while simultaneously keeping them away from powerful enemies. One of their sacred prophesies stated that the long awaited Defender would be born that year, on the twenty-fifth of the month under the sign of Pisces and on the estate of Lord Methuen. The golden child was destined to grow up to lead the defense of earth during an upcoming major offensive by the forces of evil. The Priory members knew that they needed to devise a way for The Defender to be able to locate them in order to take possession of their treasures. The papers they filed that day were filled with propaganda and misdirection. Their real purpose was, of course, not mentioned in the official documents. The registration also contained a cleverly hidden code that was meant to send a greeting and a few simple instructions that only The Defender was expected to decode.

1956 was indeed a very special year. It was a leap year, an Olympic year, and a presidential election year.

February 2: Tenley Albright won the gold medal for women's figure skating at the Olympics in Italy, marking the first time an American had ever taken that honor. Hayes Alan Jenkins, also from the United States, took home gold in the men's division.

February 21: In Montgomery, Alabama, Dr. Martin Luther King Jr. was indicted by a grand jury and stood trial for violating a 1921 law that outlawed boycotts against businesses. The charges stemmed from the arrest of 156 protesters, sympathizers, and religious clergy who had organized a city bus boycott following the arrest of Rosa Parks a few months earlier. On February 25, 1948: Reverend King had been ordained to the Baptist ministry. On this eighth anniversary of his ordination, he was handcuffed and taken into sheriff's custody. The resulting publicity surrounding the arrest and trial led to the creation of Dr. King's reputation as a powerful national figure and charismatic leader.

February 25: On the day of Ron's birth, the leader of the Soviet Union, Nikita Khrushchev shocked his comrades by renouncing his predecessor Joseph Stalin as a mass murderer and the propagator of a "Cult of Personality" that was anathema to socialist philosophy. Khrushchev's secret speech to a closed session of the twentieth Congress of the Communist Party would later be called one of the great speeches of the twentieth Century.

That spring, Bill Russell led his San Francisco University basketball team to fifty-six consecutive wins on their way to another National Collegiate Athletic Association (NCAA) title. He added an Olympic gold medal to his mantle before joining the Boston Celtics. Russell would go on to have the greatest professional basketball career of any player, in any era, winning eight World Championships in eleven years.

April 17: In Kinston, North Carolina, Jimmy Moore played Willie Mosconi for the World Pocket Billiard Championship. Moore won the coin toss and cautiously opened the match with a safety. He then sat down and watched in helpless horror over the next two hours as Mosconi slowly and methodically pocketed 150 consecutive shots. The match was over.

April 18: Proving that life can imitate art, actress Grace Kelly married the Prince of Monaco on the same day her film *The Swan* was released in theaters.

April 27: On the day that Rocky Marciano from Brockton, Massachusetts, announced his retirement as the only undefeated heavyweight champion in history, a previously unknown truck driver from Tupelo, Mississippi, took over the top of the record charts with his first hit song. Elvis Aaron Presley came to be known around the world as "the King."

July 26: The Italian ocean liner *Andrea Doria* collided with a Swedish liner the *Stockholm* off the Massachusetts coast. Fifty passengers perished in shark-infested waters.

September 4: Hundreds of bright-eyed and excited young students entered the brand-new Sandy Hook Elementary School in Newtown, Connecticut.

October 8: Don Larsen, a twenty-six-year-old member of the New York Yankees pitched the only perfect game in the history of the World Series.

November 4: The Cold War escalated as Soviet tanks rolled into Hungary in order to squash an anticommunist uprising. President Eisenhower called the attack "a brutal purge of liberty."

In the Middle East, the region erupted with conflicts in the Suez Canal and the Straights of Tiran. The events that followed eventually led to the emergence of the United States as the major outside influence in the region, deposing the European alliance between Great Britain and France from the position.

As the year neared to a close, Fidel Castro and his brother Raúl led a tiny band of forty revolutionaries in a guerrilla campaign against the government of President Fulgencio Batista.

December 27: Eisenhower proposed to Congress that economic aid should be deployed to counter Soviet penetration into other countries. This would form the basis for what came to be known as "the Eisenhower Doctrine."

Lawrence Ronald Howard, at approximately two years old

St. Augustine School and Church

1957

Duty Calls

Satan takes many forms, and one such form comes under the guise of religious extremism. In Saudi Arabia, a child is born into circumstances of wealth and privilege to respectable parents of Yemeni descent. Osama bin Laden will become known to his legions of followers as a prophet and a messiah. In the eyes of the civilized world, he will come to represent the face of evil.

. . .

March of '57 found Joe working at Andover Steam Cleaners off Bartlet Street, keeping the books, making deliveries, and so on. One morning shortly after starting out on his route he was approached by two gentlemen in dark suits who produced credentials that identified them as being attached to Army intelligence. They invited Joe to join them at Ford's coffee shop to discuss a proposal.

Their mannerisms were friendly and light, and Joe did not hesitate to agree to the meeting. He was curious about the nature of their business and had no idea what they could possibly want with him. He had been out of the service for several years now and thought that he hadn't really distinguished himself to a great degree while he served, the fighting having ended shortly after he completed his training. What he didn't know was that he had scored exceptionally high on an intelligence and personality exam that the Army had administered. He had been tagged for future consideration, should the right assignment come along.

With the courtesy of small talk quickly dispatched, the agents made their proposal. They first explained to Joe that he had been given a special high-level security clearance just to be able to hear the details of what they were going to be asking of him. After consenting to and signing a confidentiality agreement, Joe was wide-eyed.

The Pentagon he was told, had a top secret research and development program that was making serious progress in material science and in the miniaturization of electronic components. The impetus for the research was for military applications, but the market for the technology in the private sector was too important to ignore.

They told him that the president felt that it was imperative for the economy that the government should share its progress without exposing itself as the source. Joe listened in rapt silence but still couldn't see how or why he should be privy to this impressive disclosure. "Here is where you fit in," Joe was finally told. "The Weston Communications Corporation had recently constructed a massive manufacturing and R&D location on top of Osgood Hill in North Andover. We would like you to apply for an accounting position with the company. If you are hired, we would ask you to work with our couriers, acting as a technology transfer agent. You would be ferrying highly classified documents and prototypes to selected scientists and engineers at Weston's Ball Laboratories." Joe agreed to consider the proposal, and the two agents promised to contact him again within a few weeks to get his answer.

The Georgia Senate unanimously approved Senator Leon Butts's bill prohibiting Negroes from playing baseball with whites.

The Boston Celtics, with Bill Russell at center and coached by Red Auerbach, defeated the St. Louis Hawks and won their first National Basketball Association (NBA) Championship.

The Montreal Canadiens beat the Boston Bruins 4 games to 1 to win Lord Stanley's Cup.

WAHR in Miami Beach, Florida, hired a young man named Larry King to clean up and perform miscellaneous small tasks at the radio station. When one of their announcers suddenly quit on May 1, they put King on the air at a salary of fifty-five dollars a week.

On May 6 the Pulitzer Prize for nonfiction was awarded to John Fitzsimmons for *A Profile in Courage*.

July 6: In Liverpool, England, two young lads were introduced to each other at a church bazaar. Paul and John would go on to form one of the most prolific and popular songwriting teams in the annals of music.

August 17: Future Hall of Fame inductee Richie Ashburn broke Alice Roth's nose and cheekbone with a line drive foul ball while the Phillies were playing the New York Giants. Apparently attempting to finish the job, he hit her again with another hard foul while she was being carried away on a stretcher.

September 17: Sex goddess/actress Sophia Loren and producer Carlo Ponti were married in Juárez, Mexico. But neither one of them attended the ceremony. Two male attorneys stood in as "proxies" to represent the couple.

Oct 4: The USSR launched Sputnik 1, the first artificial Earth satellite. The space race had begun, and the communists were in the lead.

November 2: A UFO was seen by credible witnesses near Levelland, Texas. Several people independently reported that their car engines died when the UFO was near. The cars started back up again as soon as the object left their vicinity. This case remains one of the most baffling close encounters of its kind.

October 10: Four years after moving from Boston to Milwaukee, the Braves won the World Series, defeating the highly favored New York Yankees in seven exciting games. Series MVP Lew Burdette started and won three games, including two shutouts.

November 22: The musical duo Tom & Jerry debuted on the American Bandstand television show. They would later change the name of their act to Simon & Garfunkel.

1958

Weston Communications, Inc.

After careful consideration and without consulting Mary, Joe eventually agreed to become a field operative for the Advanced Research Projects Agency. His assignment was to infiltrate the Ball Labs facility in North Andover. In April of 1958 he began a highly successful career, rising from entry-level accounting clerk to supervisor, department chief, and finally to upper-level management at the plant with an office on Mahogany Row. Weston Communications and its parent organization, The Amalgamated Telegraph and Telecommunications Corporation (TATTCO), never knew that a handful of their employees were part of a covert program involving the transfer of advanced technologies from the government to the private sector. The initiative proved so valuable that the telecom industry alone would realize untold billions of dollars in revenues from products whose basic technologies were developed inside top secret military research installations.

As the year neared to a close, Joe received an unexpected promotion in rank from the Knights of Columbus.

In Boston, newspaper journalist William Schofield approached the city council with a proposal to link several of Greater Boston's historic landmarks together with a marked walking trail for residents and tourists to enjoy. Sixteen sites from the Boston Common to the Bunker Hill Monument in Charlestown were soon connected with a red brick line marking the almost-three-mile-long route. It became known as The Freedom Trail.

The Boston Bruins became the first team in the National Hockey League (NHL) to feature a black player: William O'Ree.

Ted Williams's Red Sox salary of $135,000 made him the highest paid player in baseball.

Rock and roll was banned in Boston after pioneer disc jockey Alan Freed was accused of inciting a riot while hosting his Big Beat show at the Boston Arena (where the Bruins played).

Vice President Richard Newhouse was physically assaulted and spat upon by protesters in Peru during his Goodwill Tour of Latin America.

The US Supreme Court ordered Little Rock Central High School in Arkansas to integrate.

Using Ball Labs patented transistors, Jack Kirby is credited with inventing the integrated circuit.

November 12: The often controversial but much beloved Massachusetts politician James Michael Curley died. He was a congressman and a governor. He also served four terms as mayor of Boston, in between serving prison terms for corruption.

Ann, John, Patricia, and Ron

1959

A New Addition

As he neared his second birthday, Mary expressed concern to the family doctor that Ron was still not talking. Dr. Shanley had advised her to take a wait-and-see attitude, as he believed that there was nothing physically wrong and that Ron was simply on his own schedule. Just because he didn't meet the milestones set by his siblings, it was not cause for alarm. That analysis proved correct. At three years old, after a slow start regarding his motor and verbal skills, Ron began to show the fleeting signs of a superior intellect.

When Ron finally did start talking, he surprised everyone by speaking in complete sentences. His vocabulary was already at the level that you would expect from a precocious five-year-old. He also exhibited the peculiar habit of whispering almost everything to himself multiple times before speaking out loud, as if practicing to make sure he got it right. His parents wisely decided not to make too much of this in front of Ron, even though some people called it odd and thought that Ron might have psychological issues. He outgrew the whispering habit before he turned six. Years later Ron would claim to have deliberately skipped the baby talk phase, waiting until he could construct whole sentences in his mind before attempting to communicate verbally.

On November 5, Mary gave birth to another son, Michael Stephen Howard. The family had outgrown their apartment in the housing project and was in need of a larger residence. All across the country, as the original tenants of these projects began to prosper in a growing economy, a major demographic trend was slowly emerging. The families of military veterans exiting the projects were being replaced by a new generation of immigrants and urban dwellers, including a growing number that would begin to accept welfare payments and subsidies as a way of life instead of as the temporary haven that they were originally intended to provide. Massachusetts's propensity or willingness to perpetuate this trend added to its reputation of being an overly generous liberal haven.

Joe had grown up in Lawrence while Mary was raised in Methuen. This presented a problem when the young couple began to shop for their first home. Each preferred their native soil. Joe thought that he had come up with an ingenious plan to solve the minor dilemma.

While Mary was still in the hospital with the new baby, Joe placed a down payment on a single-family home at 18 Odial Street, right smack on the Lawrence-Methuen town line, less than a mile from Mary's childhood home on Strathmore Road. Joe did this as a surprise, without Mary's knowledge or consent, naively assuming that she would be delighted. After seeing the house for the first time, Mary was decidedly less than impressed. She insisted that Joe should ask for the deposit back. She wanted a chance to look for a more suitable home. They ended up settling in the Odial Street location after all and would remain there for over twenty years, eventually adding two more children to their burgeoning brood.

The Irish Catholic community in Massachusetts had for several years now been supporting a young politician from Boston who had been a World War II hero. Joe was involved as a volunteer in John Fitzsimmons's campaigns for the US Congress and Senate. He worked the local precincts around Greater Lawrence, rallying support for his favorite politician. There was an air of excitement in the new home, because this meteoric candidate was now poised to become the Democratic nominee for president of the United States.

The Red Sox signed Pumpsie Green to a major league contract, becoming the last professional team to reject racial segregation in baseball. Ironically, they had been the first team to work out and consider hiring Jackie Robinson, years earlier. Their reluctance to integrate the team added to Boston's mostly unjustified reputation as a racist city.

Fidel Castro's revolution succeeded and turned Cuba into a communist country.

Alaska was admitted as the forty-ninth state.

Buddy Holly, Ritchie Valens, and the Big Bopper died in a plane crash in Iowa.

Eddie "The Big Lubanski" bowled back to back perfect games in a tournament in Miami, Florida.

Billy Sullivan was awarded the last American Football League (AFL) franchise for a team to be based in Boston, Massachusetts.

1960

A Coup for Catholics

President Eisenhower announced that he had ordered NASA to declassify top secret space-age telecommunications technology in order to make it available to the commercial sector. Of course the Pentagon had already been secretly sharing this type of information with TATTCO, Ball Labs, and a few other companies for many years.

One of the covert projects that Joe had been involved with was the development of the first telecommunications satellite. This new invention was about to jump from the pages of Arthur C. Clarke's science fiction into the domain of reality.

The battle lines for president were clearly drawn. John Fitzsimmons would face Richard Newhouse in the presidential election in November. After years of being considered second-class citizens to their English Protestant counterparts, the Irish in Massachusetts had gained newfound respect. Ron was only four years old, but even then he sensed the importance of the situation and saw how much it meant to his parents. To young Ron, the world was very much a black-and-white place where good and bad were well-defined concepts. There was little room for gray in between. And so it was with this election. John Fitzsimmons was the good guy and Richard Newhouse the bad. This notion was reinforced during televised debates where Fitzsimmons utilized the talents of a Hollywood makeup artist while Newhouse, who refused to wear makeup, looked tired and haggard. With dark circles under his eyes and sweat beading on his brow, he appeared older than his years. Tracking polls taken after the debate revealed a startling contrast. By a wide margin, the television audience believed that Fitzsimmons had clearly won the debate. The radio audience chose Newhouse. Pundits viewed the disparity as an indication that the physical appearance of the combatants was the major factor in Fitzsimmons's ability to win over the TV audience.

For reasons he could not explain or even understand, Ron did not trust Newhouse, and he often wondered how such a man could reach this level of public stature. Surely Americans would not place Newhouse in a position once occupied by the likes of Washington, Jefferson, Lincoln, and Roosevelt, would they? Ron was confident that John Fitzsimmons would win and that his parents would be very happy about it. It was important to Ron for his parents to be happy. With five children and a spouse to support, Joe Howard encountered difficulties making ends meet at times. The financial pressures would sometimes result in brief, occasionally loud arguments between Mary and Joe, often late at night when the children were presumed to be asleep. Ron would take his pillow and wrap it around the back of his head, pressing it hard against his ears in order to drown out the sounds coming from the floor below. They were able to weather the rough times as Joe's salary rose and he became more responsible with the disposition of the family's income, of which he was the sole provider.

Poker nights and trips to Rockingham Park thoroughbred racetrack in Salem, New Hampshire, were kept to a minimum.

John Fitzsimmons won the election by a narrow margin. The second age of Camelot had begun. The Howard household was ecstatic, as was almost all of Massachusetts. Irish Catholics across the country celebrated their improved social position.

. . .

While Catholics celebrated their new president, Satan plotted. If Mephistopheles were to have any chance of succeeding in his plot to conquer the planet in the next century, he would first need to render harmless the power of the Holy Roman Catholic Church. To this end Lucifer and his minions accelerated their wicked program of guiding evil men with predatory impulses into pastoral positions within the church. Diablo concentrated on flooding Massachusetts with pedophile priests, hoping that one or more of them might by happenstance corrupt and defile the young Defender before his mortal powers became too great. The identity of The Defender was at this time still unknown in the netherworld. Hell's demons had so far been able to ascertain that The Defender was born in and still lived in Massachusetts. As each day passed, they came closer to discovering him. The plan of the enfant terrible was to intercept and destroy The Defender before he was able to assume his station and fulfill his destiny.

The United States defeated Canada to win the Olympic gold medal in Hockey for the first time. The Winter Olympic Games that year were held in Squaw Valley, California.

President Eisenhower formed a secret anti-Castro-exile army, trained by the CIA.

Arthur Schawlow at Ball Labs and collaborator Charles Townes received the first patent for the development of laser technology. Schawlow would later be awarded the Nobel Prize in Physics.

American pilot Francis Gary Powers's U-2 spy plane was shot down over Russia. Powers was captured alive and taken prisoner.

Cassius Clay won the Olympic gold medal for boxing in the Light Heavyweight Division.

This concludes Volume 1

The story will continue with the future release of Volume 2, which will pick up the action in 1961.

Spoiler alert! The following pages contain random sneak preview excerpts from future volumes. Some of these sample pages are merely fragments of stories presented as teasers. For those who wish to follow this epic in proper chronological order, I suggest you wait for Volume 2.

I suspect, however, that most of you will not be able to resist peering into the future to get a glimpse of what might be in store for our protagonist in his adult life.

1994

Wild Bill

Another hobby that Ron indulged in from time to time was writing science fiction. He wrote mostly for his own entertainment and as a release and an escape from the pressures of real life. If he were to publish, he decided that he would use the whimsical pen name L. Ron Howard. Ron was not a fan of Scientology, and readers will recall how he outsmarted the Scientology recruiters in 1977 after he and his best friend Raul Pascal sat for the Master Electrician exam in Boston.

In late January, Ron attended a political fund-raiser at the Lanam Club in Andover. He listened intently while a small group of dignitaries extolled the virtues of and pondered the future prospects of the sitting governor, William Floyd Wilde. Ron was getting a little tired of hearing how brilliant Bill was, and it nauseated him to see people fawning over the governor in the hopes of tying their wagons to his anticipated presidential run. "Wild Bill," as the press liked to refer to him, was being touted as a presidential contender for the 2000 or 2004 elections. The belief within the local Republican Party was that Bill was smart enough to avoid the kind of mistakes that Michael Dukas had made in 1988. The group contained an odd mix of Republicans and Democratic Tories. They laughed at the recollection of the Duke standing in a tank, looking out of place and a bit ridiculous, wearing what looked like a fighter pilot's helmet, while being paraded in a circle for the primary purpose of being made fun of in the press.

"He was set up," remarked one hack, "and he didn't have a clue." He just stood there with that silly-looking grin on his face, wondering what all the fuss and laughter was about."

"Bill Wilde is more politically astute than Dukas ever was. His intellect will prevent him from falling into that kind of obvious trap on the campaign trail," one state rep blithely concluded.

Ron had heard enough. After taking a sip of Chivas, he announced, "I think you're giving Summa Cum Laude Bill a little too much credit." The group turned in unison to focus on the killjoy who appeared ready to put a damper on their enthusiasms. Phil Cohen, a former US congressman and the only one who actually knew Ron; challenged his view with a good-natured ribbing. The whiskey had warmed Ron's blood and loosened his lips. He uncharacteristically rose to the challenge and, in doing so, subjected himself to being the center of attention in a political drama. He was violating one of his own rules. "All right . . . I've got five dollars that say that I can set a publicity trap that Wild Bill will walk into with his eyes open. Like Dukas, he will think that he is partaking in a photo/video op designed to boost his image. Instead, he will be ridiculed in the press. It will happen on the campaign trail before the fall election. But don't worry, it will be a light enough affair that even the governor will laugh about it later. I won't actually try to damage his prospects or electability."

"I'll take that bet," state Senator Walter X. Wall interjected. The rest of the gang chimed in with their endorsement.

"OK," Ron continued, "sometime before the November election, I'll mail each of you either a five spot or a press clipping demonstrating the success of this prank." There was much laughter over the proposal, and no one but Ron took the wager seriously.

As Ron drove home he began to formulate a plan to entrap the governor in some mildly embarrassing situation. He generally liked Massachusetts's top politician and didn't want to upset him or embarrass him to any great extent. He knew that Wilde's ego and above-average intellect would make him susceptible to certain types of traps. The governor's overinflated sense of self worth could also be valuable in manipulating his perceptions. Ron sketched out a personality profile of his subject and fed the information into a computer program that he had designed several years earlier. The output was a detailed analysis that highlighted areas where the subject's personality was most vulnerable to psychological manipulation. Working in his favor is the fact that extroverts in the 125 to 135 IQ range are the most vulnerable of all. Many public individuals within this IQ range tended to have a self-conception that they were much brighter, more aware, and more important than they actually were. Ron estimated the governor's IQ fell into that range. He read the report that he had just generated and smiled. *This is going to be too easy,* he mused, *like taking candy from a baby. A six-foot-four-inch-tall baby, that is.*

The next step was to call the governor's office and pretend to be a reporter from the Boston *News-Ledger* recently assigned to cover the political scene. He employed this ruse in order to obtain a copy of the chief executive's itinerary. He carefully perused the document, searching for the right venue or event from which to set up his ambush. Ron was excited when he saw a listing for February 17. The governor was planning to spend the entire day campaigning in the Merrimack Valley—Ron's backyard. *Sweet, home field advantage, I like that!* Even better, at noontime the former prosecutor would be presenting the Crime Fighter of the Year award at Cedardale Athletic Club in Haverhill. *Oh, that's rich!* Ron drooled over the possibilities that this presented to him. As luck would have it, Ron just happened to be a member of Cedardale Athletics and was quite familiar with the place. At the time it was one of the largest fitness facilities in the United States and was just a half mile away from the TATTCO plant in North Andover. Ron knew that he would have no trouble gaining access to this event. In fact, he figured that he could largely control it.

The first order of business was to find someone on the inside who could give Ron detailed information regarding the logistics of the occasion. He accomplished this through a tried and true method. He began to romance a young lady who worked at Cedardale as a special events planner. Julie Swanson was going to be the escort who would guide the governor's entourage as he toured the mammoth facility. She would prove to be invaluable to Ron in setting up this sting, although she didn't have a clue as to what Ron was really up to. The day of the event came and Ron's plans were set. With a little cooperation from Julie, and unwitting help from Jack Goldman, the *Lawrence Sentinel* political reporter, all that was left was for Ron to execute his plan.

The motorcade following the governor around the valley arrived on time at eleven a.m. The tour began with the outside facilities first, then moved inside. Many of the club members had stopped their workouts to follow the crowd around the complex.

Ron sat passively at the bar, watching CNN while casually sipping a frozen strawberry protein drink. He appeared to have no interest in the festivities that were occurring elsewhere in the building. He nodded politely when the bartender told him that this was one of the most exciting days ever at Cedardale. Ron silently agreed, but not for the same reasons.

Adjacent to the lounge and one level lower, were three regulation-size pocket billiard tables. Ron knew from studying press reports that Wild Bill had a table in his Cambridge mansion and was a fairly proficient pool player. He played fairly regularly at the Harvard Club and rarely lost. Most of the gentlemen who frequent the club would not want to risk getting on his bad side by beating him at pool or squash. Most everyone was lobbying for something or other and would gladly pay for the opportunity to let the governor beat them at a game of his choosing.

Ron, of course, did not fall into this category, and he was capable of shooting billiards at the professional level. He strongly suspected that Wilde would not pass up a chance to demonstrate his proficiency with a pool cue in front of this crowd, seeing it as an excellent photo opportunity. With Ron still sitting at the bar, Julie sent an assistant to clear out the patrons currently using the game room. Ron then left the bar and began playing on the center table. He had promised Julie that he would throw the game and let the governor win. As anticipated, Wilde leapt at the opportunity. Julie steered the tour into the concourse next to the open-air concept game room. Seeing the pool tables, Wilde broke out in a broad smile and confidently strode into the room.

He saw a timid-looking gentleman practicing his game, seemingly oblivious to the commotion now surrounding him. "Rack 'em!" the governor bellowed, so loudly that it seemed to startle Ron. He shook Wilde's hand and introduced himself as an unemployed factory worker who had been laid off from the local TATTCO plant.

The table was racked and Ron gave the governor the courtesy of the break. Wild Bill let loose a mighty stroke and with flashbulbs popping and sent all sixteen balls scattering around the table. Unfortunately, none of them found a hole. Now it was Ron's turn. The scene had the appearance of a David and Goliath battle. On the surface it would appear that the governor had all the advantages on his side. He towered over Ron in more ways than one. He was six foot four, compared to Ron's height of five foot eight inches. Wilde was the chief of state while Ron appeared to be an inconsequential plebe—just a regular Joe, out of work and hanging around pool tables. The governor had attended Harvard and Oxford, reputedly owned a genius-level IQ, and had graduated summa cum laude from Harvard. Ron, on the other hand, had gone to the regional vocational high school in Andover and came from a lower class of Irish heritage. This Boston Brahmin was poised to teach the shanty Irishman a lesson.

As we all know by now, however, where Lawrence Ronald Howard is involved, things are rarely as they appear on the surface. The game was eight ball, and the object was for one player to sink all of the solid (1–7) or striped (9–15) balls first, finally pocketing the eight ball for the win. Ron surveyed the table and quickly formulated his plan of attack. He went after the solid balls and began eliminating them one by one, calling each shot as he went. After draining each sphere, the cue ball seemed to magically move into perfect position to set up the next shot. He also sank double bank shots and made fancy combinations.

The crowd quietly oohed and aahed as they admired the level of play that they were witnessing. The governor watched, his knuckles noticeably turning white as he gripped his stick ever tighter without realizing it. Julie began to feel uncomfortable. "You said that you were going to let him win," she whispered to Ron. "You're not even giving him a chance to get on the table, for God's sakes!" Ron just grinned and moved to the next shot.

By now, he had dispatched all seven of the solid-colored balls without a miss and had what appeared to be an easy shot at the eight ball for a certain victory. Ron lined the shot up and, while looking straight into the governor's eyes, took a blind shot and just missed sinking the eight ball. The crowd clapped politely in recognition of the run, most observers correctly assuming that

Ron had deliberately missed the last shot in order to give Bill a chance at the table.

Approximately one hundred onlookers now turned their attention to the giant, wondering if he could top what they had just seen. The cue ball was sitting on the opposite end of the table from where the governor was standing, and he briskly walked around the rectangle to survey the scene from that vantage point. A look of dismay crossed his face as he realized that even though he had seven balls to choose from, and none of Ron's left to get in his way, he still could not see any easy shots for him to take. Sounding uncertain, he called a combination shot, which he missed badly.

Ron moved quickly into place and missed again. Bill had to walk around the table for the second time, because Ron had purposefully left the cue ball on the opposite end. Still, Wilde had nothing promising to shoot at. He called a bank shot, which he didn't come close to making. He was obviously frustrated at his inability to look good in front of the crowd and the press, and it showed in his facial expressions. This same pattern continued for several more shots. Ron sidled up between Julie and the reporter, Goldman, and murmured how he was trying to let the governor win, but that Bill just wasn't cooperating. "I had heard that he was a much better player than this." Julie was uncomfortable while the *Lawrence Sentinel* reporter found the whole situation quite amusing. All through the game, Ron kept up a running dialogue with the governor. Ron told him that he thought that he had been grandstanding for publicity when he resigned from the Justice Department years earlier, supposedly in protest over the behavior of the cabinet secretary, Ed Measly. It seemed to Ron to be a vain attempt to imitate Elliot Richardson, though the circumstances were not even remotely comparable. "Since you've been governor, however, I have for the most part been happy with your administration of the state's business. I would like to support you for a second term, but first I have some reservations that need to be addressed."

Wild Bill was obviously annoyed with the constant chatter while he was trying to concentrate on his game. He was astute enough, though, to know that the audience wanted to hear the answers to Ron's questions. "And those reservations would be . . . ?"

Ron responded, "I am afraid that you are more interested in winning a second term than you are in serving it. I'm afraid that you will attempt to use your popularity as Governor to try and steal Senator Forbe's seat in 1996, or that you will lobby the Clanton White House for a cabinet position or ambassadorship. You have appeared at times to be bored with the job of governor, and I'm not convinced of your commitment to serve out a full second term."

The governor replied, "I have every intention, at this time, of fully serving my second term, if the voters of Massachusetts see fit to return me to the office, and I am not considering any alternatives."

"You see, Governor, its lawyerly language like that which makes me suspicious of your true motives. The phrase 'at this time' is there to give you an out and that disturbs me. I will, however, give you the benefit of the doubt. I'll support you for a second term with this caveat: if you attempt to leave the State House for another position before fulfilling your obligation to the people who put you in office, then I will work against you from that point on." The governor smiled weakly, while thinking to himself: *As if I've got to worry about this pool hustler working against me! He lives in New Hampshire and can't even vote in Massachusetts.* The governor realized that this little pool game was becoming a bit of an embarrassment to him and that he needed to find a graceful way to exit without looking like a quitter.

The game had dragged on now for more than twenty minutes, and Bill had yet to sink even one ball! The crowd was getting tired of hearing him complain that he wasn't getting any easy shots. For aristocats like Bill Wilde, their whole life consisted of a series of easy shots. When you are born with a silver spoon in your mouth and every little thing is taken care of for you, you may end up lacking the skills necessary to deal effectively with adversity. Bill quietly asked an aid to announce that everyone should remove themselves to the gymnasium where lunch was about to be served. Tapping himself out, he shook Ron's hand and told him to call his office sometime and they would set up a rematch, but this time it would be on the squash court, where Wilde thought that he would enjoy a physical advantage.

As the governor left to attend the crime fighter's banquet, he had no idea that he had just lost a battle against one of the best crime fighters that history had ever known.

The crowd dissipated, and Ron returned to his strawberry protein drink. *That went well!* he thought. *I just love it when a plan comes together!* In his mind, he could hear Johnny Rivers singing "Secret Agent Man." Because he was in a public setting, Ron resisted the impulse to do his customary celebratory dance to the music.

The next day he bought extra copies of the *Lawrence Sentinel*. The pool game was prominently covered and even pictured on the front page. Ron was pleased to see that, as requested, his picture did not appear with the story. He was about to clip the article and mail copies to the group from the Lanam Club, then decided against it. "They'll likely see it for themselves," he noted. Phil Cohen called Ron at home and congratulated him on his success. "I should've known better than to doubt you," he lamented. "That was brilliant!"

Honor thy father and thy mother. The Cedardale story was featured in the *Lawrence Sentinel* on February 18, as Ron had hoped and planned. It would have been his father's sixty-eighth birthday. It also marked the first time that Ron had used the L. Ron Howard pen name in public. Normally not one to drink alone, Ron made an exception as he poured an ounce of his best whiskey over ice. He held the glass high and said a silent prayer for his dear departed dad. Later that afternoon, he drove his mother to the Immaculate Conception Cemetery in Lawrence to place winter flowers on Joe's gravestone.

. . .

The amount of stress that Ron had been subjected to over the last few years was staggering. On the surface it appeared that he had weathered the period pretty well, but the cumulative effects of these stressors were gradually taking their toll. The high stress level actually served a wickedly unique purpose. It was the trigger for a series of events designed to lead Ron in a new direction. After traveling to Hell and back, and before the decade was over, Ron would be forced to emerge from his self-imposed isolation, and once he did, there would be no turning back.

Deep within his psyche, many levels below conscious, lay the conflict that was at the heart of his emotional unrest. The memory of long-forgotten and deeply repressed recurring dreams from his early childhood had been jostled and was beginning to stir, to awaken at the prescribed hour. Ron was being compelled to his destiny. He had been given a calling that he did not want, a mission that no man was capable of achieving. At night while he sleeps, his mind debated.

I don't want to be The Defender. I want to remain hidden, to live and work in isolation!

Another voice boomed in his mind in response: *Do you think that you have been given these talents, skills, and training just to stay home alone solving math puzzles! You have an obligation to use your talents in the role that you were given before the first day that you were ever born! It has all been for this! Through the centuries you have been groomed to be The Defender. Your fate will not be denied!*

Go away and let me sleep. Find someone else to be your Defender. I'm much too tired.

No! You are here to show them the way, as I have shown you.

Upon waking, Ron had a slight headache but only the faintest memory of the rancorous debate that raged in his subconscious while he slept. The conflict and the stress accompanying it did not have a sufficient outlet and consequently led to an imbalance in the critical brain neurotransmitters, serotonin, and dopamine. His brain silently switched into overdrive, with neural impulses firing faster and faster every day. Initially, this makes the brain more powerful, more intelligent. The early phase of a manic episode is where genius often shines its brightest. It is where we have seen the best from Byron, Beethoven, Churchill, Cobain, Hemingway, Van Gogh, Poe, Pollock, and who knows how many countless others who were never diagnosed.

Einstein himself had a schizophrenic son, whose affliction Albert blamed on his wife's bloodline. Einstein was reluctant to consider the possibility that the abnormal genes might have come from his side of the family. Einstein himself did not show symptoms of mental illness.

The timing of this manic state of mind could not have been more fortunate for Ron. He was making steady progress on his unified field theory, though he did not even realize how close he was getting. The extra brainpower and the high energy level of a manic episode were just what he needed to smash through the final barriers and complete the circle to find the answers to one of the biggest scientific questions of all time.

Within a few months the lack of sleep and the manic brain activity would drive Ron to the brink, with paranoid delusions and psychotic episodes. But for now at least, his genius was at its peak.

During this remarkable period, Ron was full of energy and vigor. He manically played his violin in the middle of the night and slept for only two or three hours, yet never felt tired during the day. He awoke one morning with a revelation that came to him in his sleep. He could use (Évariste) Galois's representations to count both elliptic curves and modular forms! This was the breakthrough that he needed to prove the Taniyama-Shimura conjecture! He was able to see the way clearly now, through the path to his proof.

Working almost nonstop for four days straight, breaking for only short durations, he labored furiously on his solution. He finally completed it and then tidied it up, reducing the proof to just forty-seven double-spaced typewritten pages of logically sequenced arguments. He checked and rechecked his formulas and findings until he was as certain as he could be that the paper could survive any challenge.

He had accomplished something that would set the scientific and mathematical communities on fire if they had known what he had done. He considered mailing his paper anonymously to the scientific journals but ultimately decided against it. Instead, he simply stuck it in his files under the title, "Fermat—Last Theorem—The Proof." As he wrote this, he was a little bit sad, because he knew that this was not the same proof that Fermat himself claimed, if he ever really did have a proof. No, this was strictly a twentieth-century proof, utilizing complex constructions that were completely unavailable to anyone in Fermat's time. If Fermat did indeed have a proof, it was likely to be simpler, and hence a more elegant proof than was the relative monstrosity of Ron's creation.

Finished with Fermat for now, Ron devoted his manic energies to his oscillating-string Grand Unified Theory (GUT). He spent countless hours in silent meditation, visioning himself sitting on a beam of light as it transversed the universe. In this trancelike alpha state, Ron felt that he was privy to the knowledge of the gods. They almost seemed to speak to him as revelations entered his mind from origins unknown. He called his meditation technique Telecelestial Visioning (TV).

He was making rapid and steady progress on his GUT during this period. One startling revelation after another would enter his mind. He was in awe at the level of his own production. He was distancing himself from his contemporaries by leaps and bounds. Problems that were perceived to be five and ten years away from their solutions were being cleared by Ron in a matter of days. The excitement of his findings just added more fuel to his manic furnace, and he labored night and day in pursuit of the ultimate truth. He ceased almost all other activities, stopped cleaning his apartment, neglected his bills, his family, and his friends. Clutter piled up everywhere. Reference books, magazines, and other scientific papers sat in large piles or were strewn about on floors, tables, and shelves. The Newtonian symbolism escaped Ron as a partially eaten apple rested comfortably on the top of his dresser, gleefully rotting away.

On April 2, he completed his task. He had reduced his theory to elementary principles, equations, and explanations. The culmination of all of this work led to his discovery of the long-sought master equation. From this equation (or set of equations), all of physics could be derived. The previously separate worlds of quantum mechanics and general relativity were now and forever united. The centerpiece of Ron's work was his description of the properties of a single "omnitron," the most elementary particle ever theorized.

Ron dismissed the very notion of thinking about omnitrons as particles in the traditional or classic sense. The omnitron is described as the smallest unit of energy that could be expressed using superstring mathematics. A massless particle, it was infinitesimally small. Omnitrons are what the strings in string theory were made of. Unlike strings however, free omnitrons were not constrained by the extra dimensions. They were the fundamental building blocks of the universe. And what a universe it was! While we could observe only three dimensions of space and one dimension of time, the reality is that we actually lived in a world with ten space dimensions and one time dimension. Multiple universes floated around within a mysterious common space that Howard called the univial. Ghostly particles that carry the force of gravity merrily move from one dimension to another. Separate universes engage in poetic death dances, where they eventually collide—part of a horrific rebirthing process that eliminates the big bang as a troublesome singularity and redefines the event as part of a never-ending cyclical process.

Omnitrons come in different flavors and spins and have antimatter twins. They are also the building blocks that create both gravitons and dark matter, which emanate from single-strand strings as opposed to closed loops.

All of the anomalies that affected the ultimately unsuccessful previous theories were gone. Singularities were eliminated. Black holes could now be fully described. Dark matter and dark energy were explained. Everything made mathematical sense, even if it were in a fantastical way. All of the beautiful mathematics and elegant equations that the string theorists had developed over the previous years could now be derived from Ron's work. It all checked out; Ron had accomplished what those who came before him had failed to do, what Einstein had spent the majority of his later career chasing. He had decrypted the language of God. Experimental proof would have to wait for other scientists to discover using equipment not yet invented.

At the end of his monumentally historic paper, Ron couldn't resist being a little bit silly. His last line read,

$$M = E$$
quod erat demonstrandum

Having burnt all of the physical and intellectual energy that his body was capable of producing, he didn't have much left to celebrate his incredible accomplishment. He played the Johnny Rivers song on the stereo, but there was no dancing around the apartment that day. Instead, Ron relaxed in his easy chair, surrounded by clutter, with a faint smile of satisfaction on his face. He closed his eyes and fell asleep, while the music blared, ". . . to everyone he meets, he stays a stranger . . ."

Ron knew that if he released his paper, it would be met with a lot of criticism and resistance, especially since he did not come from or was even known by the mainstream scientific community. He decided not to publish his work or subject it to so-called peer review. Not being one to revel in his accomplishments, he simply placed his completed Grand Universal Theory of Everything with his other papers and wondered what he should do next.

There was no sign that he would be called back to work at TATTCO any time soon, so Ron decided to go back into business for himself. He had tried the electrical contracting field already and wanted to do something else this time. After renting a small office in the Bay State building on Essex Street in downtown Lawrence, he began writing business plans for several entrepreneurial ventures. He decided to apply for patents for some of his more simple inventions, patents that might produce a modest income without drawing too much attention. To finance the patent applications, he would try to sell some of his science fiction stories. He would also look for investors to help finance the production and marketing of his inventions, once the patents had been applied for and were pending.

The timing for such a demanding undertaking was not going to work in Ron's favor. He had almost completely drained himself of energy, and his manic mind was still throttling him. He was about to cross that fine line where genius and madness mesh together to take their unsuspecting victim on a journey into the depths of hell. With each passing day Ron fell deeper into the abyss of madness. Paranoid delusions began to creep into his mind. He disbelieved them at first, but they kept working on him, constantly debating and offering proof for their claims. Slowly, Ron began to think that his mind might be right. The FBI could be following him; his enemies may very well have been plotting his demise. Yes, maybe even the devil himself had targeted him for destruction!

He believed that because of his heightened sense of danger, he needed to be even more cautious than he normally was. On Easter Monday, Ron had breakfast at the English Muffin diner in Hempstead but left while forgetting to pay his bill. His mind was polluted with irrational thoughts, and he was having trouble concentrating on driving. By the time he got to Lawrence he was in full panic. He stopped his van next to the police station and went inside to ask for help. With all of the commotion going on inside the precinct, Ron was unable to think. Distressed, he ran outside. He headed down Essex Street, unsure what to do or where to go. On the sidewalk he saw someone whom he thought could help him. He rushed toward the Catholic priest and gushed, "Father! Father! Please help me! The devil is after me and will take me to Hell! Please help me!" The priest grabbed the large cross that hung around his neck and thrust it toward Ron. Apparently he had mistaken Ron to be one of the devil's own minions, and he was trying to repel him. The priest chanted in Latin as Ron tried to explain to him that he posed no threat.

A Lawrence police officer noticed the altercation and stepped in to diffuse the situation. Ron knew that the cop wasn't going to buy his "the devil is after me" story, so he did not tell it. He simply stated that he was asking the priest for help because he was exhausted and confused. The Irish cop kindly asked Ron if he could help him, and Ron gladly accepted the offer. He agreed to be taken to a local hospital. After a short examination at Lawrence Memorial, he was sent to McLean Hospital in Belmont. Following a night of observation there, Ron was transferred to Wingate Hospital in Latham where he was eventually diagnosed as suffering from an isolated manic episode. Ron had no history or previous indications of any psychiatric disorders. His family history also did not contain any evidence of mental disease.

He protested being sent to Wingate and insisted on being taken to Hempstead Hospital in New Hampshire instead, because it was less than a mile from his home. He thought that he would be more comfortable and less anxious there. He assumed that since he had medical insurance that he should be able to go to any hospital that he wanted. But he was being held in protective custody by the state of Massachusetts for his own well-being, and as such, it was required that he stay in a Massachusetts facility.

Ron managed to survive his twenty-eight-day stay in Latham, though he later described this time as a visit to the depths of hell. He returned home refreshed, intact, and unbroken. His mettle was now completely forged by fire. He survived that nightmare so that he could live to face even more dangerous times. Looking back, Ron realized that the prophesy of his life, given to him in a series of childhood dreams, was coming true. While he was in the hospital, lying awake at night, the conflict in his subconscious had begun to move into his conscious mind. In the darkness of the locked isolation ward, Ron was surrounded by poor souls beset with demons that wailed throughout the night. The devils were especially active during the night of the full moon. In this environment, Ron didn't have the strength to fight his calling, and he finally surrendered all resistance as he resigned himself to the fate into which he was born. Upon release from the psyche unit, he was a man on a mission like never before, convinced that he was and would forever be The Defender.

November 4: Governor Wilde won reelection to a second term by the largest margin in Massachusetts gubernatorial history.

1995

Destiny

Ron was out of work for most of the year. He spent his time writing science fiction and developing business plans. He also took post-graduation courses at Southern New Hampshire University, which, under the rules in place at the time, allowed him to collect extended unemployment compensation without requiring him to look for work. He was relaxed during this period and achieved a sense of well-being that had previously eluded him. He knew that he was here to fulfill a glorious destiny. He did not feel worthy or even capable of this station in life, but he now accepted it without question or reservation. He was consumed, however, with finding out exactly how this destiny was supposed to take shape or how he was supposed to shape it.

. . .

Mary had been having a difficult time since her husband and mother passed away within six months of each other. She occupied her days and dealt with the grief in a variety of ways, primarily by spending time with her children, their spouses, her eleven grandchildren, and with friends and relatives whom she had nurtured relationships with for decades. As another sign that her family was blessed, the grandchildren had all arrived in an incredibly predictable fashion. After the fifth grandchild, John was the first to notice the pattern of boy, girl, boy, girl, boy. This sequence, though notable, did not seem so remarkable at the time. But when the pattern continued, unbroken through eleven births, it became downright eerie. Ann and her husband, Mike, had two boys and two girls. John and Valerie had one girl and one boy. Patty and Dan had two boys. Ellen and Rob had one of each while Elizabeth and her husband Bill had a girl.

. . .

Ron kept a close eye on the governor of Massachusetts, and he didn't like what he was seeing. His original suspicions had proven to be true. Wilde had been more interested in winning a second term than he was in serving it. He announced that he was going to try and unseat the incumbent junior senator, Jerry Forbes. Ron was not pleased with this betrayal, and he began to build a dossier full of information about the governor. If he decided that the situation warranted it, he would work behind the scenes to ensure that Wild Bill would never again be elected to high public office. Wilde had made a formidable adversary in the diminutive Howard, and he had no idea that by neglecting his duties as governor and announcing that he had no intention of finishing his second term, he had also sealed his fate. If Lawrence R. Howard decided to work against you in an election, you were likely to end up behind the eight ball.

In October, Ron was finally recalled to work at TATTCO. This time he was assigned to a shop that made state-of-the-art transmitters, receivers, and transceivers for the convergence of cable television, telephone, and internet signals all being carried over the same cable or twisted pair. The products were ahead of their time and were scheduled for trial installations in Southern California.

. . .

At Templeton Textiles, Alan Firestone's luck finally ran out. On December 11, at 10:13 p.m., the humidity in Flock Line One dropped to a dangerous level. An electrical grid arced out, and a fireball ignited the nylon fibers that were floating in the air. The fire roared for several seconds before being apparently extinguished by the overhead sprinkler system. With the Methuen Fire Department on its way, smoldering remnants soon caught some fresh air and flames reappeared, which began to climb an interior wall. By 10:30 the fire escaped its containment and moved through the ceiling and into the floorboards on the next level. The exterior of the buildings were brick, but the interior support beams and floors were all wood. Much of the floor space was soaked with oil, because the moving parts of the textile machines threw off oil that was used to lubricate them. By 10:42 p.m. the entire main mill building was ablaze. Alan Firestone's worst nightmare had come true.

Osama bin Laden continued his Holy War against the United States with the bombing of a military training facility in Riyadh, Saudi Arabia. Five American servicemen were killed in the attack.

1996

A Split Personality

Fortunately, some say miraculously, no one died in the Templeton Textiles firestorm. Three out of the five buildings in the complex were destroyed, and a handful of employees were critically injured. At the time, it was one of the largest industrial fires in the history of the United States. Alan Firestone, apparently fearing bad publicity and an onslaught of lawsuits against the company, began to launch a preemptive strike even as the last of the flames were being subdued. Firestone boldly declared that he would rebuild his factory on the same site, and that he would keep all of his employees on the payroll for as long as he had the funds to pay them. The strategy successfully muted his critics while propelling him into the national spotlight. The man who could have and possibly should have prevented this tragedy was now seen as a great hero in light of the unquestionable generosity of his response.

· · ·

TATTCO announced that beginning in 1997 it would split itself up into three different companies. They would spin off their computer division, formerly NCAR, and its telecom equipment manufacturing division, formerly Weston Electric. The parent company would remain as a long-distance carrier, pursuing a growth strategy in data communications, networking, and CATV while simultaneously trying to break into the local carrier markets after an exclusion period expired. It was perceived that the telecom equipment company would fare better as a separate entity, because many of its potential customers were competitors of TATTCO. They were reluctant to purchase the equipment from TATTCO because of a perceived conflict of interest. The divestiture was viewed as the best way to remove that obstacle and in turn wake a sleeping giant.

Ball Labs would accompany the manufacturing division, giving it instant worldwide credibility. The labs were an enormous asset that TATTCO never seemed to fully appreciate.

. . .

Ron's brother Michael Howard quit his day job as a social worker for the state of Massachusetts in order to concentrate on his karate school full time. A third-degree black belt, he had opened the school two years earlier, after teaching classes for free at the Lawrence Boys' Club for six years. Ron had interested Michael in the Asian art of self-defense back in the late sixties, and Michael had pursued his training with an almost religious fervor. Ron took his self-defense skills off-line in 1976, just as Michael began to study formerly. Ron had hoped that Michael would open a karate school someday, and that he would be Michael's partner and first student. Michael didn't quite know how to decline Ron's offer to help him establish the school, and he remained noncommittal for months until Ron finally got the hint. Ron was hurt by this rejection but knew that his penchant for keeping secrets and not allowing others to really know him was a factor leading to Michael's decision. The recent episode of mental illness was also likely to have been part of the thought process. Ron quietly accepted the slight as one of the many negative consequences that would inevitably follow as a result of the life path that he had chosen to take. In the end, Ron had to admit that Michael had made the correct decision. Michael built his self-defense business into a thriving enterprise, and he did it without requiring any help from his brother. Ron was very proud of Michael's accomplishments and took a small measure of pride himself in the knowledge that he had planted the seeds that played a role in Michael's career choice. The National Karate Institute in Salem, New Hampshire, specialized in teaching children life skills that go way beyond self-defense. Legions of parents would testify with high praise that Michael helped shape the character of their children in a positive fashion.

. . .

The forces of evil had come a long way since the dark ages. They now used modern, sophisticated techniques to achieve their goals. One of their primary directives was to gain control of numerous properties in the corporate world. Access to the money and power that was concentrated there would be one of the keys to winning the war that was approaching like some dark storm cloud. The Emperor of Evil sought small victories on his way to winning larger battles. One such victory occurred at the Reebok footwear company. A despicable demon named Incubus surreptitiously convinced gullible and naive executives at the company to name a sneaker line after him. It turned into a public relations disaster when it was later revealed that Incubus was a demon who is known to descend upon unsuspecting women to rape and molest them while they slept. The product line was quickly recalled by an embarrassed management team a few months after its worldwide release. A satanic rock band later found success using this ugly name with the 1999 release of their album entitled *Make Yourself*.

. . .

Almost right from the start of his second term, Bill Wilde gave every indication that his present and future interests lay elsewhere. After dancing like a maniac at his second inaugural, Wilde seemed to have no energy left to put toward governing the state. In the first five months of 1995, Wilde traveled constantly, not in his role as Massachusetts's governor, but as Pete Winston's finance director. Instead of visiting Great Barrington, Massachusetts, in the aftermath of a devastating tornado, Wilde flew to Los Angeles to work on Winston's presidential campaign. The Boston *News-Ledger* began tracking the governor's travels in a daily "Wilde Watch" feature. Radio stations played a game called "Where's Wildo?"

Ron considered Wilde to be an embarrassment. Clearly he had misled the voting public in regard to his post-election plans. The last straw was drawn when Wilde filed papers to run for US senator. In Ron's opinion, Wilde had intentionally failed to honor his responsibilities as governor and would have to pay a steep price for deceiving the good citizens of the Commonwealth of Massachusetts.

Ron closely monitored the senatorial campaign. He sent an anonymous letter to Jerry Forbes's staff outlining the areas where he thought that Wilde was most vulnerable. He specifically highlighted comparisons of Forbe's military career and heroics to Wilde's use of his student deferment to apparently avoid the draft. Young men from the aristocratic class were not expected to risk their lives in mortal combat in some rice paddy halfway around the world. That honor was generally reserved for the lower classes. Jerry Forbes was a rare exception to that rule. He stepped up to volunteer after graduating from Yale and became a naval officer.

The election was lost for Wilde when one of his loyalists tried to smear Forbes military service record by implying that Forbes had received his Purple Hearts through less than honorable circumstances. The backlash knocked Wilde down ten percentage points. His wounded and ill-conceived campaign never recovered. Attempting to vacate the governor's office so soon after winning reelection had hurt Wilde's chances more than he thought it would. Ron hoped that the election loss would result in Wilde's buckling down to refocus on the job that he was being paid to do. His hopes, however, were short-lived. Wilde was simply determined to find another job for himself, and, if the citizens of Massachusetts wouldn't give it to him, then maybe someone else would. Wilde shamelessly lobbied the Democratic president for a cabinet-level position—attorney general, commerce secretary, whatever—it didn't matter as long as he could get away from the drudgery of pretending to tend to the state's business.

The White House rebuffed his efforts, but tenacious Bill still wasn't finished. Unlike his pool game against Ron back in '94, he just didn't know when to quit. He now saw himself as ambassador material. After preliminary discussions with Will Clanton's State Department he decided to pursue the opening for Mexico. When Ron heard that Bill was trolling for an international assignment within the State Department, he laughed out loud. Of all of the personal attributes that come to mind when thinking of Wild Bill, the word "diplomat" never entered his mind.

Ray Finnegan, the former Boston mayor who was the US emissary to the Vatican was currently driving the Clanton administration crazy with his decidedly undiplomatic approach to the job. *You would think that State would be leery of another Irish politician from Boston joining their diplomatic core in light of their* recent experience with Finnegan, Ron thought. He knew that Wilde wouldn't stand a chance at winning any ambassadorship. Ron already had a plan to stop him, and all he had to do now was implement it.

Jasper Holmes, a staunchly conservative Republican from North Carolina was the sitting chairman of the Senate Foreign Relations Committee. Bill Wilde was the kind of Republican in Name Only (RINO) that made his blood boil. For Wilde's nomination to go forward, Holmes would have to schedule a hearing for his committee to vote to recommend that the nomination be moved to the floor of the Senate. Ron put together a videotape of snippets from various news sources that he had been collecting for several years. Everything on the tape demonstrated that Wilde's political ideology ran counter to Holmes's conservatism. Furthermore, when asked during the senate campaign if he would vote for Jasper Holmes as chairman of the Foreign Relations Committee, Wilde responded, "Holmes was not my kind of Republican."

Ron included this clip on multiple occasions, spreading it liberally throughout the tape. On issues such as abortion, drugs, and tobacco, they were on opposite ends of the political spectrum even though they were both members of the same party. There was nothing on this video for Holmes to like; in fact, it enraged him so much when he watched it that he threw a paperweight through the television screen in response.

Despite constant pressure from several high-level sources and organizations, Holmes steadfastly refused to schedule Wilde's hearing. Seeing that his nomination was in trouble, Wilde used the impasse as a convenient excuse to depart from the job that he was no longer interested in performing. With a level of arrogance that is his trademark, Wilde stated that he was resigning from the governor's office in order to spend the summer in Washington fighting for his nomination. He was quitting, he said, not because he had become bored with the job, but so as not to "hold the people's business hostage . . . to the politics being waged in Washington." *How freakin' noble!* Ron thought facetiously. *Good luck and good riddance; chump! I hope that you have a backup plan when the summer is over, for I believe that you will be returning empty-handed.*

Wilde was a welcome sight to the Washington press core. Witty and glib, he played politics in a style all his own, and he provided some much needed comic relief to the scene. Despite good press and intense pressure from all sides for Holmes to move the nomination forward, Wilde's prospects never improved. Ron knew that if there was anyone in Washington who could withstand the arm-twisting without caving in, that man was Jasper Holmes. He had the power to keep Wilde in his place, and he was going to exercise that power in full. Wilde eventually realized that the battle was lost, and as summer neared to a close, he asked President Clanton to withdraw his nomination. Wilde returned to the Bay State as Ron had predicted, empty-handed, unemployed, and with his tail between his legs.

After striking out three times in a row, Wilde decided to go find another game to play. He signed on with a Boston–New York law firm, then rented a cabin in the woods where he "wrote" a mystery novel, something about fishing for mackerel at midnight. For someone who majored in classics at Harvard, this would appear, on the surface at least, to be less than a literary masterpiece. The book was released in 1998 and fell like a lead sinker right to the bottom of the discount bins.

Life could prove to be a very difficult game to play, especially when you were not given easy shots to take. Just ask Billy Wilde. It was a lesson that he is still learning. William Floyd Wilde was still a relatively young man. He would likely resurface in Massachusetts, New York, Texas, or on the national political scene. When and if he did, Lawrence Ronald Howard would be waiting. There would be no more easy shots for Bill Wilde to take.

. . .

Around this time Ron began sending his science fiction stories to agents and publishers. His work was unanimously rejected. He realized that he needed to think about ways to differentiate his brand of sci-fi from the rest of the industry.

. . .

The output from ARPA's laboratories had been steadily declining, and Ron was informed that budget cuts were the reason. He suspected otherwise.

. . .

Ron had a vague notion (from his formerly repressed dreams) that there was some kind of hidden message waiting for him to discover. In this dream he saw fragments of an event from long ago. A castle perched on a mountaintop was enveloped in white clouds. The eerie scene floating in his head included a church and a graveyard. A man in a black smock was on his knees on the floor of the church. He opened a door in the floor and then disappeared below it carrying some parchments in one hand and a chalice in the other. Ron saw the roman numerals one, nine, five, and six on the parchment. The handsome mystery man then reappeared above the floor and closed the trapdoor behind him. Standing upright now, he placed his left index finger over his lips and closed his eyes. The dream then dissolved.

In his attempt to try and find clues to his destiny and the meaning behind his strange dreams, Ron decided to go back and start a methodical search from the beginning. He researched world history records for the year of his birth, 1956. It bothered him that he had no idea what he was looking for. He just hoped that he would know it when he found it. After spending months examining various historical archives, he finally came across a story that seemed to resonate with him. The obscure reference mentioned that a group of prominent aristocrats and businessmen had filed papers in Annemasse, France, to incorporate a formerly secret society known as the Prieuré du Notre Dame du Sion. The listing in the French directory was placed under the subtitle "Chivalry of Catholic Rules and Institutions of the Independent and Traditionalist Union."

After reading about the 1956 event and the many mysteries that this society had purportedly been involved in over the centuries, Ron suspected that this was something that he needed to know more about. The story was full of religious intrigue and skullduggery. The mystery centered on the small village of Rennes-le-Château, in southern France. This captivated Ron; he was intrigued by the prospects of ancient secrets, hidden treasures, and encrypted codes that surrounded this fascinating conundrum. *Is this the same place that I saw in my dreams?* Ron asked himself.

———※———

The government of Sudan finally bowed to US pressure and expelled Osama bin Laden from the country. Bin Laden was able to elude capture by US agents however, and eventually found refuge with the fundamental Islamic Taliban government in Afghanistan. Proving that his operations had not been impeded, a truck bomb exploded outside the Khobar Towers in Dhahran, Saudi Arabia; nineteen American soldiers lost their lives in the assault.

1998

The Data Vault

During the spring of '98, Ron conducted a highly unusual experiment. Spurred on by the failed efforts to get his sci-fi stories published, he had spent much of his free time in 1997 developing an expert system, an artificially intelligent computer program designed to suggest outlines and advice that could be followed with the goal of producing wildly popular fiction.

The program analyzed data from a large sample of best-selling fiction across all genres. The input was carefully assembled to meet the necessary criteria to ensure that the sample was sufficiently representative and unbiased. Sales and average review ratings were registered for each title. With the maturation of the Internet, full text copies of the most popular novels were readily available in digital format at reasonable prices. Many were in the public domain.

The output of the program consisted of formulaic outlines designed to help the writer produce popular fiction. The emphasis was on salability, with scant consideration for literary merit.

The topic of sex was deliberately left out, because it was deemed too obvious. The program took fifty-three hours of computer time using massively paralleled processors. The 1997 version of a supercomputer involved the stringing together of a large number of average desktop workstations in parallel, in order to duplicate the equivalent amount of processing power previously available only with access to multimillion dollar proprietary mainframe systems. Ron put his worldwide network of Phoenix Foundation secret agents to work in unison in order to construct his virtual supercomputer. After the results came in, they were verified using a series of redundant, independent, crosscheck algorithms.

Ron was both pleased and slightly troubled by the results. They just happened to agree with his own notion of what would make good, commercial fiction. This in turn led him to suspect that his personal biases must have crept into the programming and the sample selection, despite the extensive measures he employed to avoid this anticipated problem. Confused and unsure of himself, he took his data to MIT to seek the opinion of an old acquaintance, Dr. Herbert Talman. Professor Talman was impressed with Ron's work; he and Ron both expressed surprise, considering the (relative) simplicity of the task, that no one else they were aware of had attempted to do this. Several researchers in the music industry were already experimenting with computer programs that were capable of composing original new songs, so the vague concept was definitely in the air. Apparently no one yet had thought to adapt those techniques to designing fiction. After studying and analyzing Ron's program, samples, and data, Dr. Talman confirmed that the program was clean and that the sample was indeed sufficiently large, representative, and unbiased. The results could be trusted with 98.643 percent certainty, within two standard deviations, accompanied by a confidence limit of 0.08. Talman marveled at Ron's program, delivering the ultimate compliment when he used the word "elegant" to describe it.

The output listed several outlines that were good prospects for the model of popular fiction that Ron was seeking. Each concept was scored with a number between -1 and 1. Ranked at the very top of the list, the program highlighted specific mixes and percentages of religion, science, and politics as the best chance for producing a blockbuster novel. Christianity, with its history of conflicts, violence, mystery, and hidden secrets came out as the most promising religion to exploit. Hidden codes, messages, and buried treasure also scored high as ancillary features. Outlines for subplots were also delineated.

The battle between good and evil, seraphs and demons, as fought by their human counterparts, was at the center of the stage. The formulas could be applied with equal success to historical, modern, or futuristic fiction. The program provided suggestions for structure, pacing, plot points, character development, and even the number of words per book.

Ron was pleased that the results allowed for the possibility of a rich diversity of work, meaning that the formulas could be applied to many different story outlines. He had been worried that it might produce a recommendation so specific that it could only be applied to a very limited number of stories. A secondary group, not nearly as powerful as the first, identified numerous other generic guidelines that added to the potential for producing a large range of popular fiction.

Once Ron had completed this phase of the project, the next step was to apply the formulas and create original fiction based on the computer-generated guidelines. As a fledgling science fiction writer, he had many ideas that he could use to produce test cases. He started in this direction, but before long he had a brainstorm involving an even better, less biased testing methodology. Ron was aware that his own creative writing and storytelling skills were not highly developed. He conceded that there were many professional writers who were capable of doing a better job with his formula than he could.

Ron wrote fiction as a hobby, not a profession. Theoretically, a relatively unknown but talented and imaginative professional should be able to break away from the pack of midlist authors with the help of Ron's data. Ron's quest now was to find a writer whose background fit the selection criteria. He needed to find a novelist who was new or unknown but had already demonstrated the ability to secure a publishing contract.

Ron didn't have to look very far to locate a promising subject. One of the engineers at Ball Labs, Billy Buckman, recently had his first novel, *Virus*, published as a mass-market paperback. Ron stopped him outside the TATTCO cafeteria one day and introduced himself. He congratulated him on his success and they made some small talk. Ron then inquired if he was interested in meeting for lunch sometime. He told Buckman that he had used an AI program to develop promising outlines for popular fiction. "I think it suits your style well—so if you are interested, I could show you in more detail what I'm talking about and how it might help you grow your readership." Buckman brushed off Ron's overture, telling him that he worked out at Cedardale during his lunch break every day, and he didn't have any free time on his schedule. Ron wished him the best and bade him good day. Buckman had no idea of the magnitude and life-changing potential of the offer that he had just passed up. Ron continued to find someone else to give his fiction-writing advice to.

The next opportunity presented itself in April when Ron read a story in the *Lawrence Sentinel* about a local high school creative writing teacher who had just published his first novel, a techno thriller called *The Data Vault*. The next day, Ron went to the Hempstead Public Library and pulled the new release from Don Breen off the shelf. He sat down at a table and polished it off in about two hours. *Perfect,* he thought. *He's got all the attributes that I need for my test case.*

Searching the AltaVista website, Ron found that his target would be making a public appearance in Salem, New Hampshire, on April 21.

At the reading, Ron purchased a copy of the hardcover, then took a seat in the back row of collapsible metal chairs. He was late. He glanced around the room that had been sectioned off for author appearances. Around forty chairs were set up, but less than twenty people attended the event. Some of them were likely friends or relatives of the newly minted writer, Ron assumed.

After some opening remarks about the NSA, the author performed a short reading from his novel. He then asked if the audience had any questions for him. Three hands were immediately raised. The third question inquired about his future plans. He announced that upon the publication of his first book, he had received a contract for three more titles. He stated that he was currently working on his second book, *Betrayal Boulevard.*

"So, if anyone has any good story ideas . . ." He only half jokingly offered. "I'm open to suggestions." He smiled. The audience laughed.

The celebrated author then invited everyone to come forward if they wanted to talk or have their copy autographed. A few people left. Ten lined up in single file waiting for their turn to greet the author. Ron stayed in his seat, reading the *New York Times.* He glanced up and saw about five people remaining in the line. A few minutes later everyone had gone except for the two principles in this drama.

Ron approached with an outstretched hand. "Mr. Breen, Sir, I had to come here and tell you how much I enjoyed your book. It's an excellent first effort. I'm aware that it takes a little while for a new fiction writer to build a readership, but I'm sure that you're going to do very well!" The writer modestly deflected Ron's superlatives. They chatted for a few minutes before Ron steered the conversation toward the craft of writing. Ron offered some advice. "You're trying to break into a genre that is already saturated and well served by Tom Clancy and others. What I think you need to do is differentiate your work to a greater degree. Try to find, invent, or revive a genre that is underserved and then endeavor to become its champion." He mentioned a computer program he had been working with which produced outlines and recommendations for popular fiction. Ron first talked about broad themes. He suggested, "Within the conflicts and confluences of religion, science, and politics, there lived an explosive mix of literary possibilities. The battle between good and evil, seraphs and demons, as waged by their human surrogates, is rich with market potential. When properly combined, this approach has enormous potential in the marketplace."

Ron provided a few more details, being careful not to overload the writer with information. He finished by pointing out a plot point that Satan often poses as the Holy Spirit and tricks his minions into believing that they are doing God's work. Ron mentioned that he himself was writing in this mixed genre, which he called "techno-political-supernatural sci-fi" and that samples of his work could be found on the AnEx Publications website.

"I'm predicting today that within a few years you'll be at the top of the best-seller lists! One last piece of advice: "Keep writing smart—don't let editors, publishers, or agents convince you to dumb down your work in an attempt to appeal to a wider range of readers." The author was wide-eyed and appeared to hang on Ron's every word. He asked questions and seemed genuinely interested.

The effect of the conversation was designed to be mostly subliminal, and too many details would negate that effect to some degree. They had talked for fifteen minutes or so before Ron presented his copy of *The Data Vault* for the writer to sign. "I'd like you to date that page, because in a few years, after you've had that major best seller, I'm going to come back and remind you of our conversation and the prediction I made today!"

The author smiled. "OK!"

When Ron returned to his van in the parking lot at Barnes & Noble, he wanted to dictate some notes regarding the phase of his experiment that he had just completed. He was excited because he thought that the meeting had gone exceptionally well, and he was anxious to record the event for his journal while all of the details were still fresh in his mind. Removing the micro-cassette tape recorder from his suit coat pocket, he was about to push the record button but noticed that it was already running in voice-activated mode. Apparently he had accidentally recorded his entire conversation with *The Data Vault* author. He rewound the tape and then played it back while driving home. *Sweet! I can make my notes later!*

With the signing of Pedro Martinez, Ron was excited about the prospects for the upcoming baseball season. The team looked sharp in spring training and Dan Duquette promised that they would be able to compete in their division. The Yankees and Orioles were thought to be the teams to beat in the AL East that year. Ron hoped and suspected that the Sox were going to give them a run for their money.

Alan Firestone had succeeded in leveraging the good will that was created by keeping his employees on the payroll after the fire. He secured government guaranteed loans and had special legislation enacted, giving him attractive tax breaks and incentives to keep his manufacturing in Massachusetts. His PR campaign has also been successful in minimizing the post disaster litigation that normally follows such situations. All Firestone did was make sound business decisions designed to manipulate the situation to his greatest advantage. For that he is proclaimed to be a national hero; some called him a saint. He eagerly accepted the moniker as he traveled around the country on a speaking tour, receiving awards and preaching to others that they can be as great and generous as he is.

US embassies in Kenya and Tanzania were victimized by car bombs. The death toll was listed at 224 people. Osama bin Laden's organization Al-Qaeda was implicated, according to the CIA. The government increased the reward for information leading to the arrest of bin Laden to five million dollars. He was placed at the top of the FBI's Ten Most Wanted fugitive list." Despite all of this, the name Osama Bin Laden was still unknown to the vast majority of American citizens, because most didn't pay close attention to these events until they hit home.

2003

Leonardo's Cipher

Ron turned the page of his newspaper and glanced at the best-seller listings from the previous week. At the very top was a new release entitled *Leonardo's Cipher* by Don Breen. His suspicions aroused, Ron purchased the book the next day and immediately took it home to read. After a short while, he placed the novel down by his side, hands trembling.

The messenger has arrived!

In a sign of her approval for the restoration of the Sacred Feminine, an impressive image of the Virgin Mary appeared in the window of a Catholic hospital in Milton, Massachusetts, on the very day that *Leonardo's Cipher* was released.

A week later, as Ron was driving through a morning rain on Route 111 heading east, the radio station interrupted programming to cover a breaking news story coming out of Franconia Notch. The announcer's voice boomed out of the rear-mounted speakers: *"After maintaining his sentry for over ten thousand years, the Old Man of the Mountain has collapsed and . . ."*

Ron slammed on the brakes and swerved to the right, tires screeching. He abruptly parked his van in the breakdown lane. *I can't believe this is really happening!*

Jumping out of the truck, he neglected to close the door. Walking briskly through the woods that paralleled the highway, his whole body trembled in fear as the gravity of the situation hit him with full force for the first time in his life. He remembered a prediction from the disturbing recurring dreams of his childhood as he stopped and looked toward the sky for guidance.

"On the morning when the old man falls from the mountain, the messenger will be on top of the world, and you will know that the time has arrived for you to . . ."

Walking back to his truck, soaked from the rain, Ron began to overcome his fear. Wiping tears from his eyes, his emotional conflict gradually gave way to a steely resolve. A 180-degree turn headed him in the direction of Route I-93 north. *It's time to join forces with the Leader!*

He parked in the lot beside 295 McArthur Street in Manchester. The sky had cleared and the sun was burning bright. The elevator lifted him up slowly and deposited him on the third floor of the old mill. Greeted by a vision of an angelic-looking young woman shrouded in a beam of intense white light, he struggled to find his voice. "Puh-puh-pardon my appearance," Ron stammered while his eyes slowly adjusted to the backlighting, "I . . . ah . . . I got caught in the rain. I'm Lawrence Howard. I'd like to volunteer to help with the campaign."

"Welcome aboard, Mr. Howard, we've been expecting you." Katherine Murray replied, flashing a radiant and knowing smile.

Massachusetts State Attorney General Bob O'Reilly announced that his office had completed a sixteen-month grand jury investigation into the handling of the Catholic Crisis by the Boston archdiocese. His office regretfully reported that they were unable to prosecute the case against the church hierarchy. The ninety-one-page report detailed instance after instance where pedophile priests were routinely transferred from parish to parish with little or no regard for the children who were being placed in harm's way. Problems with the statute of limitations and with old laws that exempted the church from having to report the crimes prevented any meaningful prosecution of the offender's enablers. O'Reilly made it clear that the scope of the crisis was much larger and ran deeper than had been previously reported. Victims numbered not in the hundreds but in the thousands over the six decades covered by the investigation.

Whether by luck or divine intervention, St. Augustine school and church in Lawrence was one of the few area parishes that remained unscathed by the scandal. Predatory priests were never able to penetrate this fortress, despite many attempts to gain entrance. This was largely due to the strong management practices of Father Edward P. Carney, OSA. Father Carney was an old-school fire-and-brimstone preacher who ruled St. Augustine's with an iron fist. If the archdiocese of Boston had been run by Father Carney instead of the weaker souls who had possessed the office in the latter half of the twentieth century, the crisis would not have been allowed to flourish. Cardinal Law, his predecessors, and even the Vatican had fallen victim to one of Satan's most common ploys.

The Holy Spirit and Satan speak to us all on a daily basis. Satan, however, often will speak in the voice of the Holy Spirit in order to trick his victims into doing his despicable work. The Catholic Church had fallen deeply and globally into Satan's insidious trap. For decades The Holy Roman Catholic Church from Rome to Boston and beyond had listened to the devil and had blindly followed his instructions on how to deal with the pedophile problem. The Catholic Faithful were horrified and outraged when the extent of the problem became completely clear. The vast majority of everyday parishioners knew perfectly well how to distinguish between the guidance that they receive from the Holy Spirit and that of the devil in disguise. They could not understand how the Church leadership had strayed so far from common sense and the wisdom of the Holy Spirit. Many parishioners believed that if they were to be assured that this could never happen again, then the church needed nothing less than a revolution in order to right their ship of souls.

Ron was saddened to learn that the scandal had resulted in a crisis of faith regarding one of his close relatives. His cousin Miranda Howard had been a devout Catholic who taught Sunday school at St. Augustine's in Andover for over three decades. She now openly renounced her faith. Miranda was adrift, searching for a new and better religious affiliation. Ron attempted to counsel her to return to her native religion and to join him in his efforts to achieve reform. She rejected the overture and continued on her own journey of religious exploration, bouncing from Catholic to Jehovah's Witness to the Baptists, constantly searching for the truth. Ron had always considered her to be someone of very deep and unmoving faith. It turned out that her faith was just intense, but not deep; it rested on a foundation of sand, and she was easily turned adrift, capable of being blown away from the truth like sand in a windstorm.

Ron felt that he had to do something. The events of the last two years convinced him that the church had lost its way. He established a vehicle to carry the message of his vision of revolution and called it the Roman Catholic Reformation Organization (RCRO). He set up a website at RCRO.uno in an attempt to incite a revolution of change whereby pressure from communicants all over the world would force church leaders to adopt radical reforms. It was immediately controversial. Lauded by the left and condemned by the right, the vast majority in the middle didn't know what to make of it. The RCRO membership grew slowly but steadily as intended. Rome, as everyone knows, was not built in a day. The transformation that Ron and his followers sought would take much time and patience to achieve.

2004

The Columbine Memorial

In the 1990s Lawrence Howard and his Phoenix Foundation organization started an international campaign to combat the emerging "cyber-squatting" problem, where people register Internet domain names with the intention of reselling them for a profit. In general terms this was a perfectly legal transaction. In certain instances, though, either the legality or the morality of such activities were highly questionable. In the early days of the World Wide Web, it wasn't always clear if trademark protection applied to domain names.

If a company like Coca Cola wanted to set up a website for CocaCola.com but found that the domain name was already owned by someone, they would sometimes decide to pay a very large sum of money to the person who had registered the name. The alternative was to file an expensive lawsuit claiming that since Coca Cola was their trademark, then the person (i.e. the cyber-squatter) who registered CocaCola.com should surrender the domain name and transfer it to the Coca Cola Company.

Because a trademark-infringement lawsuit could take years to wind its way through the federal court system, and the company was in a hurry to get their website up and running, this gave the cyber-squatters a lot of leverage. Cyber-squatting in many instances was used almost like a form of extortion or kidnapping, with the cyber-squatter demanding that the person or company pay a ransom to get the domain name that they might actually have a legal right to anyway. It was a legal gray area for several years. Defendants might successfully argue that the trademark owner had sufficient time to register the name themselves, and by failing to do so in a timely manner, they had effectively given up their rights under the applicable statutes. When companies fail to take action to protect their trademarks, courts have sometimes ruled that those trademarks have reentered the public domain, making them available for others to claim or employ them.

Howard thought the questionable side of this whole business was unseemly. He decided to use his computer hacking skills and his worldwide network of Phoenix Foundation secret agents to work against some of the world's most notorious cyber-squatters. He and his agents put notices on numerous computer bulletin boards (the social networking sites of that time) asking for people to contact them if they were being subject to extortion attempts or were in the negotiation phase of engaging with a cyber-squatter. The Phoenix Foundation stated that they might be available to help people and companies deal with their issue at little to no expense.

When contacted, Howard would evaluate the situation on a case-by-case basis. Sometimes he would just act as an arbitrator and help the plaintiff negotiate a fair price, often much lower than what the plaintiff might have paid without his assistance. But if he decided that the situation was unseemly enough for more serious intervention, he would employ the Robin Hood solution.

In this scenario, Howard or one or more of his agents would hack into the domain registration account of the cyber-squatter and transfer the domain name to whomever he believed was its rightful owner. This usually was done in several steps, routed through VPN's with disguised IP addresses and moved through third and fourth parties so that the transaction could not be traced back to the source or blamed on the person or company who ended up with the property.

What Howard despised most were scenarios where a cyber-squatter attempted to profit from a personal loss or tragedy. That is how he came to be associated with the Columbine Memorial.

Mr. Robert Easton, then chairman of the Columbine Memorial Committee had a problem. The committee needed to set up a website to inform the public that a design and location for their memorial was set and that they needed to raise funds to finance the project.

To their consternation, they found that every attractive and reasonable website name was already taken, having been registered by numerous cyber-squatters from around the world, some who were demanding payment for the website names that they essentially were holding hostage. Unfortunately, this was completely legal.

Mr. Easton and his committee were determined not to give in to these demands. The money that they were allowed to spend needed to go into the memorial itself, not the hands of these loathsome profiteers.

Easton and other committee members consulted lawyers, judges, and anyone else of note who might be able to help them find an alternative to paying the price that the virtual extortionists were asking for. At every turn they were told that their options were not good. They might have a slim chance in court, but the process could be long and potentially costly in itself. They also would probably lose the case, because "Columbine Memorial" was not yet a trademarked name.

Unwilling to give up, Chairman Easton searched the Internet for possible alternatives. Despite performing a thorough and exhaustive search, all he could find was a small and obscure organization called the Phoenix Foundation, based in Massachusetts. They seemed to be the only reference to anyone offering to help a person or organization deal with a cyber-squatter issue without going to court or charging a high fee.

Mr. Easton contacted Howard via e-mail and then by phone and inquired if he could hire the foundation and, if so, what the costs might be. After learning about his plight, Howard assured Mr. Easton that he would take on his case pro bono and promised that the likelihood of success was high. Mr. Easton directed Howard to keep in touch with his secretary and report to her if he made any progress.

Incensed and angered that people would try and profit from such a horrific tragedy, Howard made this case his top priority and put all of his resources to work on it. Within a month's time, Howard and his agents had purchased, seized, or otherwise gained control of around a dozen domain names, including the top three most coveted and prized ones: ColumbineMemorial.org, ColumbineMemorial.com, and ColumbineMemorial.net.

Howard was excited to pass on this good news to Mr. Easton's secretary. Frankly, he would have preferred to present it directly to him, but for whatever reason Easton had decided that it was something his secretary should handle. Looking back, Howard now sees that this was a hint that Mr. Easton possibly wasn't ranking this task as high on his own priority list as he perhaps should have.

But that was just Howard's opinion, and he could be wrong, of course. He called the secretary and explained to her what the Phoenix Foundation had accomplished and what he was offering to do, which was to transfer all the domain names he had acquired over to the memorial committee, free of charge. The young lady did not quite understand what he was saying, though. Inexplicably (to Howard, anyway) she replied, "Oh, we've already tried that and could not get them." Before Howard could straighten out the miscommunication, the secretary had hung up on him. Flabbergasted, he sent her an e-mail attempting to correct her false notions and tried to underscore the importance of the issue. In response, she sent a reply dismissive of the e-mail, which demonstrated that she still didn't grasp the meaning of the message that she'd likely given scant review if she actually read it at all.

Ron had to assume that the secretary had never been informed that her boss had enlisted the Phoenix Foundation to help with the problem. He got a little testy at that point. Having spent considerable time and effort to achieve this very worthwhile goal, he was perplexed and slightly annoyed at the reaction he was getting. He sent another e-mail to the secretary and cc'd it to Mr. Easton. The e-mail stated that the foundation had gone to great lengths to secure ownership of these domain names, and that if in fact they did not truly want them, Howard would seek out another community group in Littleton, Colorado, to transfer them to. Chairman Easton promptly called Howard, apologized for the mix-up, and stated that they did indeed wish to accept the offer to transfer the domain names over to their control. Once again Howard was asked to work with the secretary to complete the domain name transfer process.

Mr. Easton and his committee never inquired how Howard came to possess the properties, nor were they overly active in their efforts to thank him or the Phoenix Foundation for what they had done for them, which was fairly substantial. That was actually OK with Howard, because he didn't do it for reward or recognition. But, being human, he did think for a second or two that if he were in their position, he would have conveyed his gratefulness a little more effectively and earnestly, and it saddened him that they seemed to take his actions for granted. It wasn't a matter of Howard needing their appreciation so much as it was his disappointment in them for not offering it. Howard held himself and others to high standards, and sometimes he did it to a fault.

"I guess I just wished at the time that they had better manners is what I'm trying to say," Howard was quoted in one interview. "I'm sure Miss Manners would agree that the situation called for a written thank-you letter on the committee's letterhead, signed by one or more of their prominent officials. I imagined that there were probably many others who did not receive proper thanks for their contributions to the effort in getting the memorial funded and built."

Howard quickly got over that minor negligence. "My personal satisfaction is derived simply from the knowledge that I did a good thing and not from any expectation of thanks or reward. These are obviously very good people, doing good work themselves, so if they were a bit too preoccupied to realize or recognize the importance of what we had done for them, I can and do forgive them for that. A few years later, I did get invited to the dedication ceremony, but that appeared to be due to the fact that my name popped up as a thousand-dollar-or-higher contributor, because I had also made a cash donation to their fund in addition to the domain name dealings."

The following paragraphs contain more quotes from the Lawrence Sentinel interview with Lawrence Ronald Howard.

> **Lawrence Sentinel:** Exactly what was the process you followed in this case?
>
> **Ron:** First, I identified all of the domain name variations that I believed the Memorial Committee should seek. Then I searched the registration records to find out who had

registered these names and what their contact information was. Some had used private registration services, which masked their identities and made the task of finding out who they were much more difficult.

With this information in hand, I assigned a few of my best secret-agent volunteers to hack the private registration databases and connect the dots to identify the persons or companies who were using a private registration service to hide their identity. The next step was to contact the numerous cyber-squatters involved and tell them that I was acting to secure the domain names on behalf of the Columbine Memorial Committee.

Some were open to negotiation and agreed to allow me to purchase the names from them at a semi-reasonable price. I don't actually consider *any* price reasonable here, as I believe it is absolutely despicable for anyone to attempt to profit from this tragedy. But in order to facilitate the process, I held my revulsion in check and treated these individuals in a respectful manner, which was no small feat. One gentleman did agree to give us the domain name he registered if we just reimbursed his expenses.

Some were not open to dropping their asking price by much, forcing me to execute plan B. Well, OK, they didn't actually force me, I decided to execute plan B (which might have been sort of illegal) of my own free will, and I was willing to suffer the consequences of those actions, knowing that my conscience could handle it.

So we hacked the accounts of the remaining cyber-squatters and transferred their Columbine Memorial–related domain names into anonymous accounts. Then we called them and told them what we had done. We informed them that they were free to file complaints or lawsuits against us. We counseled them to carefully consider the potential ramifications, considering that their complaint would be a matter of public record. I told them to be prepared to suffer universal worldwide condemnation and disdain for having attempted to profit from an enormous tragedy. As anticipated, no complaints were filed, at least none that I am aware of. If complaints were registered, then no one in power saw fit to investigate or prosecute those complaints.

We eventually obtained and offered around a dozen or so domain names to the Columbine Memorial Committee in Littleton, Colorado. The one name I recommended that they use as the primary domain was ColumbineMemorial.org. But I counseled them that *all* of the names had value and that once in their possession, they could own and control these names in perpetuity. I informed them that there were at least three good reasons for them to accept the transfer and take ownership of *all* of the domain name variations that I had secured on their behalf. By variations, I mean slight misspellings, or hyphenated versions, like Columbine-Memorial.org, and so on.

The first reason that holding *all* of the names was a good idea was the fact that some people seeking to find their website were likely to try one of these other names in their browser and that it was in their best interest that, whatever name the user entered, it got them right to their website on the first try. All of the domain names could be set up in such a way that they all pointed to or were automatically forwarded to the primary site, ColumbineMemorial.org.

The second reason was that there were already numerous websites out there commemorating or memorializing, in some fashion, the Columbine Tragedy. Some were legitimate memorials to the students who were killed, and some of the sites were operated by scammers seeking donations. So when people performed search-engine attempts with the word 'Columbine' in it, they were given lots of choices on the results page. By registering and using several different name variations, the Committee could ensure that more than one search-engine response or result pointed to their official website, lessening the chance that they would be lost in the clutter or that an interested party might end up sending their donation to a scam artist.

The third and equally important reason was that if they failed to register *all* of the names that I had secured and placed into 'protective custody' for them, then those names could eventually be used by unscrupulous persons to set up phony Columbine Memorial websites.

Chairman Easton or the committee declined to take this advice. They only accepted two of the dozen or so names I had recommended and secured for them. Those two were ColumbineMemorial.org and ColumbineMemorial.com, which were very successful and are still in use today. The unfortunate part is that the rest of the names eventually saw their registrations expire because the memorial committee was not interested in owning them, and I had moved on to other cases and was not paying attention to their renewal cycles and had let them lapse. The other domain names were and still are susceptible to be picked up by less than honorable individuals for dishonorable purposes. This could easily have been prevented if I had continued to renew them or, more appropriately, the committee had acted on my advice.

All in all, though, I was very happy with how the case turned out, and I hope that the Columbine Memorial Committee was satisfied with our work and contribution to their efforts."

Note: After this interview, Howard recovered ColumbineMemorial.net and placed it back into the protective custody of The Phoenix Foundation. If the memorial committee changes their mind and wishes to own it, TPF will transfer it to them.

2007

The Trask Affair

The following story is a firsthand account (taken from Lawrence Ronald Howard's personal journal) of his involvement with a famous court case.

Note from the author: This document (journal entry) has been edited to remove any mentions of the contents of the final settlement, the public disclosure of which was prohibited by the court in the consent agreement. Mr. Howard is free, however, to discuss most of the events that led up to that settlement.

Excerpt from Howard's journal entry:

Sometimes my cases are brought directly to me by people with problems, as in the Columbine Memorial story, or one of my Phoenix Foundation secret-agent volunteers brings it to my attention. Otherwise I personally seek out and find cases or situations to work on myself or to assign to an agent or a team of agents. My antenna is always up, because I never know when or where something that comes to my attention might contain a potential case or present a problem that I'd like to attempt to solve.

I like to fight against injustices, and sometimes a situation comes into view where I see an opportunity to possibly do some good and make the world a slightly better place. That is how I came to be (somewhat reluctantly) involved in a famous lawsuit against Daniel Trask. The lawsuit generated headlines around the world in 2007.

As previously stated, I usually try to work behind the scenes and keep my cases secret or at least very low profile. This is one of the cases that got away from me a bit and spilled into the media mainstream. Because it is or was prominent in media circles, I would like to explain it in detail, since the media reports didn't quite get it right.

As I grew older, I began to notice how pervasive and sinister the problem of age discrimination in the workplace really was. I saw good friends and other competent, hardworking middle-aged acquaintances and close relatives having an increasingly difficult time finding gainful employment after losing a good job in a down economy. It became obvious to me that many hiring managers routinely (and to an alarming degree) were dismissive of older job applicants regardless of more relevant factors.

The problem is extremely difficult to prove and to fight on an individual basis. That is why it has become so commonplace and why I call it sinister. It's devastating to millions of individuals, to society, and to our economy. Little is done to correct the situation, and it's not talked about often enough.

Despite his obvious flaws (and don't we all have them?), I like Daniel Trask, and I like his television show *The Candidate*. I watched and enjoyed the first season and the second. When the third season started, it struck me that a consistent pattern was being followed, and I found this pattern disturbing. Every single one of the finalists with a chance at a high-level executive position at his company was under the age of forty! Statistically speaking, this could not be a random occurrence; I believed that it had to be due to a deliberate pattern of preference. Empirically speaking, numbers just don't fall that way in an unbiased random distribution from an applicant pool of over a million candidates.

I reasoned that *The Candidate* was different from all of the other reality television shows in one very important regard. That difference involved the prize that was awarded to the winner.

Instead of the typical reality show prize, the reward on *The Candidate* was very unique. When the show was over and the cameras were turned off, the winner of the show was given an employment contract for at least one year as a full-time, high-level executive within one of Daniel Trask's companies, with a salary of $250,000 and the possibility of extended employment within the organization. Indeed Mr. Trask himself often referred to the show as "a sixteen-week job interview."

This was no fake reality show job! It was a real-life golden-ticket opportunity to work in a real job in Trask's commercial property development company. And it was a really, really good job! It should be open to qualified candidates of all ages. It struck me that, on the surface, it appeared that Trask's on-air hiring practice had to be subject to the same employment laws that human resource professionals and hiring managers are required to follow. But given my nature, I didn't just assume this to be true—I performed due diligence and thoroughly researched the issue before coming to a final conclusion.

I broke out the law books and studied the applicable federal, New York, California, and Massachusetts state statutes that applied to this situation. I scoured the law libraries in Boston and on the Internet, trying to find a precedent that would allow the parties involved in producing Trask's show to have any viable claim to being exempt from these hiring laws. After an extensive and exhaustive search, I failed to find any legitimate reason or precedent that would allow the show to exclude a protected class in the process of hiring someone for *The Candidate* job.

In legal terms, what Trask needed in order for his show to be exempt from certain employment laws was a bona fide occupational qualification (BFOQ). This would be something found in a job description that would clearly necessitate or allow discriminating against a protected class.

In Trask's high-end hotels, for instance, he might have a position titled "Men's Room Attendant." Since this job involves working in the men's room, cleaning and handing out towels to men who are using the facilities, Trask would be allowed to discriminate on the basis of sex. He could advertise that the job was only open to male applicants, and he'd be within his legal rights, because there are good (bona fide) reasons to exclude women from this applicant pool. Certain physically strenuous jobs, such as firemen and policemen (or -women) have age restriction limits for new applicants, which have held up in court as meeting the legal definition of a BFOQ. In a scripted drama for television or movies, if a part was written for an African American man, the casting people could legally discriminate on the basis of color and only interview black males. But this wasn't a scripted drama—it was a vehicle to hire someone for a management job that started after the show was over and the cameras were turned off.

What I noticed about Trask's applicant pool was that *every* single one of the finalists selected to compete for *The Candidate* job in season one, season two, and season three were in their twenties or thirties and that not even one of them was over thirty-nine. So out of an applicant population that Trask's own publicity had said was over a million aspiring candidates, the show apparently had deemed that not *even one* of those applicants who were over forty were attractive enough as candidates to advance to the finalist level and get a chance to compete for the job on television. But men and women at age forty and over are a protected class as established by the Age Discrimination in Employment Act (ADEA) of 1967.

It was quite apparent that the show was establishing and exhibiting clear and irrefutable evidence of an apparent preference (bias) toward younger applicants and a total exclusion of members of the protected class. This meant that potentially thousands of applicants were illegally discriminated against. Moreover, older executives watching at home and seeing the demographic makeup of the finalist groups would be discouraged from applying for future *Candidate* interviews, seeing that there appeared to be a preference for younger executives.

My next step was to download application materials from the show's website. I was looking for the job description or anything else that could be construed as any type of claim of the need for a BFOQ where the job given to the winner would somehow require someone younger than forty to hold. Or perhaps a disclaimer that the primary purpose of the show was for entertainment and that the winner would simply be paid for participation on the show and not for performing a real-life job after the show was over.

But I found nothing there that would allow them to exclude this protected class. All statements indicated that the winner would end up in Mr. Trask's employ and receive a year's salary for performing the duties of the job that was won as a result of appearing on the show.

For anyone to have the qualifications for an upper-level executive position in Trask's corporation, you would think that many of the most qualified applicants would be highly experienced ones with many years of increasing responsibilities in real-estate development or related fields. You would think that *many* of the most qualified individuals would be over forty years old.

Continuing my research, I decided to check out the makeup of the applicant pool for season four. I noted the locations, dates, and times when the auditions and interviews for season four applicants were going to be held, and I visited three large cities on the day of these auditions. At each of these sites, I found long lines of men and women dressed in smart business attire, holding briefcases and folders with résumés and work samples. I counted the number of people in the lines and did an estimate of those whom I believed looked to be clearly older than forty years old. I videotaped the lines as I walked from one end to the other with a portable video camera. I then interviewed several people at each site and asked them their age and several other questions.

Virtually everyone I talked to believed that the show did indeed appear to be more interested in featuring younger persons than older ones. When I asked the applicants who had identified themselves as being over forty if they thought they had a fair chance of winning *The Candidate* job, most answered something to the effect that, even though it was an uphill battle to overcome the perceived age bracket preference (that they also perceived was in play), they hoped that their experience, charm, and personality would work in their favor and allow them to overcome that potential roadblock. Many of them also agreed with my speculation that many older workers who otherwise would have liked to apply failed to do so because they were discouraged upon seeing that the finalists' pool in each season was completely and totally skewed toward younger applicants.

In order to bring an age discrimination lawsuit to court, one needed to establish a standing in the case, usually by being one of the aggrieved parties yourself; that is, you need to be someone who was directly discriminated against. At this point in time, I had no standing and, more importantly, before I got to the point of considering legal action, I wanted to give the Trask organization a chance to rectify the problem themselves. I devised what I thought was a great plan to achieve this while at the same time establishing standing as a backup if the original plan didn't work out to my satisfaction.

I attended an interview for *The Candidate* just outside Boston, Massachusetts, armed with this pitch. I told the interviewer that what sets my candidacy apart from the hundreds of thousands of other applicants was that in addition to being highly qualified, based on my résumé alone, I could also potentially save Trask and his organization a ton of money and avoid a huge impending headache: namely by preventing or preempting a lawsuit that could potentially run damages in the tens of millions of dollars.

I explained to the interviewer that the show appears to be in direct violation of the ADEA and that they needed to protect themselves against a potential class-action lawsuit by changing direction and beginning to accept a more representative mix of applicants into their pool of eighteen finalists. Continuing to (apparently) express a preference for younger job candidates for an executive position at the wholesale exclusion of a protected class was foolhardy, especially when the remedy was so easily accomplished, and the potential damage for failing to act was so great. Further, I made the case that if I had been on Trask's team when the show was in the preproduction stage, I would have made sure that this problem was addressed right from day one before any episodes aired.

I believed that I made an excellent presentation but knew that it fell on deaf ears. When it came time for my interview, I was escorted into a large conference room with around a dozen other job candidates. I had to fight for time to speak, and the interviewer seemed to not be interested in much of anything I was saying. I got the distinct feeling that she had been instructed on what type she was looking for, and after the first glance, she knew I didn't fit that type and so nothing I was going to do or say was given any weight. She was, of course, just a casting agent, not a professionally trained Human Resources department hiring manager.

The applicants were interviewed in groups of ten to fifteen, and each group was told to stay close to their cell phones after they left. Some candidates will be called back for second interviews being held the next day. If they didn't get that callback message by nine p.m. or so, that meant that they had been eliminated from consideration for the job.

I did not receive a callback, so I made a follow up call myself, then sent an e-mail and a letter to Trask's headquarters, once again detailing what I could do for them. I explained that I thought the show was in the hands of "entertainment auditioners" who were not accustomed to having to comply with most employment laws because no other reality shows involved giving someone a real job as a prize, and most entertainment or acting jobs had BFOQ's, allowing them to discriminate against otherwise protected classes on the basis that actors had to fit the role they were being considered for.

I pointed out that Trask's own lawyers had apparently failed to properly advise him to make sure they didn't give the impression that they were routinely excluding protected classes from the applicant pool. I also pointed out: "Had I been in your employ at the outset and during the planning stages for this show, I would have very strongly advised you to include more than a token sampling of applicants over the age of forty in the group of televised finalists. That would have protected you from giving the appearance of discrimination and possibly exposing you to serious class-action litigation. Clearly, you need someone like me in your organization looking after your interests, because your current staff and legal team failed you in this important regard."

After these earnest efforts all failed to produce results or even generate a response from Trask or his organization, I decided that it was time to turn up the heat. I would make sure that I received Mr. Trask's full attention and that he would know that this was a serious issue. Now that I had been interviewed and rejected, I could be considered as an injured party who had obtained legal standing to pursue a claim and make the case for a class action to seek relief for all of the potential plaintiffs.

To prevent the court system from being overrun with frivolous lawsuits, federal law required that ADEA complaints be first submitted to the Equal Employment Opportunity Commission (EEOC). I wrote the complaint and submitted it through registered mail. The case was assigned to the lead investigator out of the EEOC's regional office in Boston. He examined my documents, deemed that the case potentially had merit, and officially opened an investigation. He sent out letters of inquiry to Trask's office, Mark Bayliss Productions, and the NBC television network. They were all informed that the EEOC was investigating a complaint. A demand for information on their hiring practices was made, and a deadline was imposed for a response.

Upon completion of the investigation, the lead investigator produced an opinion stating that he found the complaint to be valid and the evidence of illegal discrimination compelling. He determined that the case had merit, was not frivolous, and strongly advised that it should proceed to court.

At that point, I decided to request a Right to Sue (RTS) order from the EEOC. This would keep the case in my hands, and I could control the settlement negotiations. If I didn't pursue this avenue and the EEOC brought the charges directly to court and the complaint was granted class-action status, I would lose all control over the matter.

I was concerned that the EEOC might overzealously prosecute the case and that the defendants would be punished to a much higher degree than I was comfortable with. It was imperative that I maintain central control over this operation, since it was I who had conceived and pursued it to this point.

The RTS was granted without delay, thanks to the strong backing of the EEOC's investigative officer. That RTS order started a ninety-day clock ticking—I had ninety days to file the lawsuit or lose all rights to pursue the claim any further. If I could settle the claim with the defendants before that ninety-day period expired, then the whole thing could be kept quiet and outside the public's knowledge, which was my preference.

I have a long history of fighting good fights and not allowing the media or the public to have access or knowledge to the goings-on of my activities or Phoenix Foundation missions. I've never had a desire to be famous. I believe that would hurt my ability to accomplish many of my goals, and the dark side of fame is definitely not appealing to me. There are good things that can come from being famous, but on balance, it is a distasteful way to have to live, in my opinion.

Wasting no time, I wrote to Trask and Mark Bayliss (the show's producer) and advised them that I was in possession of the RTS order and that I was preparing the case for submission to federal court in Boston. I advised them that I was open to negotiation and that I hoped we could come to an agreement that would keep the case out of court.

This time I succeeded in getting their full attention. Trask hired the prestigious New York law firm of Kater Munchousen & Rosencrantz, LLP. The case was assigned to a prominent attorney, Merrill Mahoney, who sent me a registered letter and asked if I would call him to discuss the matter.

I found Mahoney to be a man of great integrity. He was both highly professional and surprisingly candid, especially after we had established a good rapport and mutual respect as a basis for our ongoing negotiation.

I let Mahoney know right away that my purpose was to use this situation to raise awareness and bring media attention to the problem of age discrimination in the workplace. Trask's status as the biggest celebrity businessman in the world ensured that both the media and the public would pay attention if he championed this cause. I explained that this was not a money grab and that we could attempt to structure a settlement that would not damage Trask or his reputation. Indeed, if we played this right, it would enhance Daniel Trask's reputation as he became a leading advocate for older workers. In addition to generating publicity for antidiscrimination awareness, I would also seek to have Trask end the pattern of discrimination that the show was exhibiting.

I laid out my case and demonstrated that this was not really about me having being rejected as a candidate. I was simply one foot soldier leading the charge. This was a class action where the potential lawsuit would represent *all* of the applicants who were over forty years old who appear to have been summarily dismissed and who (it appeared) never stood the same chance as their younger counterparts to compete for the executive-level job at Trask's corporation.

I made it clear that this case was about advocacy for the protected class and that I would not be seeking large monetary or punitive damages. I only sought a remedy and publicity for the cause and nothing for myself. One remedy could be for the show to proactively seek out and feature candidates over forty, fifty, and sixty years old in future seasons. The law, of course, does not require companies to go out of their way to recruit members of protected classes; it simply does not allow them to discriminate against them when they do show up and apply for the position.

Secondly, I wanted to see Daniel Trask become a leader and a champion of the cause, extolling the value of and the virtue of hiring older workers and imploring businesses to not look past this experienced and highly valuable section of the workforce. With the aging of the baby-boom generation, it was even more important today than ever that age discrimination in employment be looked upon as an evil that needs to be exposed and railed against. It knew it would never be conquered, but significant and incremental progress could always be made.

Since the show had such an abysmal record of not appearing to welcome older job candidates, I did not believe that it was too much to ask for them to step up and do some advocating and recruiting themselves. This could happen without the public ever knowing that there was a potentially large class-action lawsuit that had spurred the defendants to start featuring some older candidates and also making public statements or taking other actions that raised awareness of the problem.

I also stated that, even though I had a very solid case, I would not seek to overplay my leverage and extract anywhere near a maximum price from the defendants. I said: "You are fortunate that I am the one who is bringing this to you, because someone else would almost certainly try to squeeze your clients much harder." I reiterated to Mahoney that one of my key points was that I did not believe that his clients did anything intentionally evil here, and as such, I could not in good conscience exploit my position too far. I told him that I had caught his clients (who I believed are good people) in a vulnerable position, and I was attempting to use that fact to do a public service.

Mahoney seemed very receptive to my suggestions and appeared relieved that I was willing to settle the case quietly out of court without attempting to extract a high price. I was offering to forgo a monetary settlement, avoid any embarrassment for his clients, and do a public service all at the same time. It had the potential for the settlement to be a win-win situation for all parties involved. Daniel Trask could emerge from this as a hero for extolling the virtues of older workers and causing hiring managers around the world to rethink their practices.

From that point on, our negotiations were very polite, civil, and had the distinct air that we were working together to get something worthwhile accomplished for the benefit of society, while protecting the defendants from serious damages. If I had pursued the claim to the max and the jury had ruled in my favor, the court might have awarded monetary damages to every *Candidate* applicant who was over the age of forty. This could have potentially amounted to civil and punitive fines in the tens of millions of dollars. I was quite confident that had we gone to court and proceeded with discovery, I would have

1. Found a sizable group of qualified applicants who were over forty years old who were routinely

dismissed from the applicant pool, nearly always at the very first screening.
2. Likely found that the casting people who were doing the initial screening of the over one million applicants had been given directions on the type of candidates being sought and that type was likely to be biased toward the younger job applicants.

Even though the negotiations with Trask's high-powered attorney were going extremely well and appeared headed toward an amicable settlement, we still only had that brief ninety-day window to deal with.

I believe that I had done such a good job at putting Mahoney at ease with the case that he lost sight of the critical need to get the settlement done and signed before the impending deadline. So when that deadline approached and the settlement papers had not yet been drawn up, I was forced into a very difficult decision.

If I let the Right to Sue order issued by The EEOC lapse, I would lose any ability to see the claim through to what I imagined would be a righteous and just settlement. If I did file the case in federal court, that would continue to protect my leverage, but the downside is that it would become a very public affair, which is something I had tried hard to prevent. At this point I really didn't see any alternative but to proceed to court, because if I didn't, then all of the hard work done up until that point would have been for nothing. The defendants would not have any motivation or need to do anything that I was asking of them, and the case would die without my having accomplished any of the goals I had set.

I wrote the lawsuit myself without any assistance from or consulting with any attorneys. I filed it in federal court and braced for the expected onslaught of attention from the media. And what an onslaught it was! I was deluged with media requests. My phone rang constantly for days. Every major media outlet reported on the story, and most of them asked to interview me. TV trucks lined up on my street, and I fled to the safety of my sister's house to hide. I received requests to appear on numerous television and radio shows. I am publicity shy by nature and politely declined the vast majority of these requests, even though I could have worked them to my advantage and profited from the exposure. I did agree to a few telephone interviews, starting with the Associated Press (AP). I thought it was important to get my points across before the opposition had a chance to paint me in an unflattering light. I was fully aware of Trask's penchant to come out in the media with guns blazing if anyone challenged him or attempted to embarrass him.

The story went global within two days of the court filing, and it was reported in over one hundred different countries. The AP article was translated in numerous languages. Every major news and entertainment outlet covered it, as well as thousands of other venues. It was a business story, an entertainment story, a case-law story, and an ethics story; it touched a chord with an incredible number of different constituencies across the board. Law professors called and told me that they were using it as a case study in their classrooms and that the celebrity angle ensured that the students found an otherwise boring topic to be highly interesting. All this is exactly what I was hoping for, except for the public exposure I received. I was thrilled, however, that people were more aware of the issue now and were talking about it.

Age discrimination in the workplace was receiving the attention that I sought, and I was very pleased with that aspect. The story ran in newspapers, magazines, and on television and radio. It received more media coverage than any age discrimination lawsuit in history, mostly because of Daniel Trask's high-profile status in both the business and entertainment industries.

When I agreed to the telephone interview with the Associated Press, I thought that this was the best way to get the story correctly told to the widest possible audience. I attempted to explain that the story wasn't about me being some disgruntled, rejected reality show applicant. I tried to strike home the point that I was just a small figure in a much bigger picture. I explained that this was a class-action lawsuit and that the main point was that *The Candidate* reality series was a job interview and candidate selection process that demonstrated a wholesale bias against an entire protected class of applicants from around the entire United States. I repeatedly stated that I was merely one plaintiff (the lead plaintiff) in the class action and that the story should focus on the exclusion of the protected class of applicants as a whole and *not* on whether or not I was selected or rejected.

I told the AP reporter, "I'm just the first representative of *all* of the aggrieved parties to step forward. If the case continues, potentially thousands of plaintiffs may be added, and they will all be equal participants on the same footing as me. This actually has very little to do with the fact that I was not a successful applicant and everything to do with the fact that I believe Daniel Trask's televised selection process is illegally discriminating against an entire class of job seekers who are over forty years old. As each season airs, and the bias becomes more and more obvious, thousands of other older applicants are discouraged to even attempt to apply, knowing that it appears that they are not valued by Trask's organization or his show." I was frustrated by the reporter's narrow line of questioning focusing on me, and I suspected that the reporter had already made up his mind before the interview even started as to what slant he was going to present.

So when the AP story broke, I was not surprised that the reporter failed to get it right. He had thrown out journalistic integrity and unbiased reporting in favor of sensationalizing the story and painting it as being mostly about one disgruntled reality show reject striking back at "The Daniel."

The Associated Press lost a chance to be a messenger that age discrimination in the workplace is a plague in this country and that it should no longer be a tolerated, hidden problem. They went for the tabloid headline and story instead, and shame on them for that.

After that bad experience, I did not speak to any more national news outlets. I conducted phone interviews with my local newspaper and one of the Boston dailies. My local newspaper, the *Lawrence Sentinel* did the best job of reporting the story, but it was the poorly written AP version that was reprinted or broadcast around the world.

Even though my hometown paper did right by the original story, they subsequently wrote an editorial asking the judge to throw out the case. It was a laughable, pro-business-slanted request from the right-leaning editorial page editor, because it would require the judge to ignore both the evidence and the law!

In my next conversation with Mahoney, I expressed my sincere regret that we had been unable to get things done before the time line had necessitated that I file the lawsuit, which caused a bit of unnecessary embarrassment to his clients. Mahoney let me off the hook and apologized, stating that it was his fault because he had gotten busy, and then, with the holiday season and all, the deadline had escaped his view. We agreed that we would continue to work in good faith on the settlement and that in the interim Trask would not make any disparaging comments in the media against me, as Trask is very prone to do whenever he is challenged or sued.

When asked about the lawsuit, Daniel Trask released this statement: "We have had very few people over a certain age apply to be on the show. If they did and we liked them, we would love to cast them on the show."

I was happy that Trask did not lash out with any harsh words against me, but I cringed at the statement, because it was so poorly conceived and potentially damaging to Daniel Trask's defense. Once again, had I been in his employ I could have counseled him and prevented him from releasing such an ill-conceived response.

I told Mahoney that he should advise Trask to either keep silent or at least have a competent attorney vet his public statements on the matter. There were two big things wrong with Trask's public response to the lawsuit.

1. It appeared to acknowledge that his show did indeed have a goal and a desire to be inclusive of the protected class and came close to inferring knowledge of liability if discrimination had taken place. That statement just about killed what little chance he had in court, because the only viable defense against the overwhelming evidence that his selection process was biased was to freely admit the bias and claim that it was actually much more about entertainment than it was about hiring someone for a job. He'd have to claim the right to a BFOQ allowing him to

"cast" whomever he wanted to fill the "roles" of the eighteen candidate finalists. It's a pretty weak defense, given the circumstances, but it was virtually the *only* defense left available to him. And he just about obliterated that avenue with his two-sentence response to the lawsuit.

2. What exactly did he mean by "over a certain age"? What age? *Ninety?* The *only* age that mattered in this court case was forty and over. So he appears to be saying that he barely gets any applicants from the protected class! And since I already had irrefutable evidence that he had lots of applicants over forty, this claim of having "very few" was ludicrous. I could have made him look silly in court when I had him on the witness stand to defend that claim. I would be playing the videos from the lines of contestants and asking him if he could point to any of these "very few" individuals who appeared to be "over a certain age." I would constantly pause the video at every person who appeared to be over forty and ask again and again if this was one of the "very few." I would ask him to define what numbers fall into his conception of "very few." I would ask the jury if they thought that a hundred applicants was "very few." Is a thousand "very few"? I also would have been given, during the discovery phase, copies of all of the application forms and taped auditions from the first six seasons, with further irrefutable evidence of qualified older applicants. I'd have a large stack of applications and videos on display while repeating the question: "Is this very few?"

What are the chances that some of the jury members would be over forty themselves and would have experienced age-related job discrimination at some point or knew someone who did? Statistics said the odds are very good that some of the jury would fall into that category. And, of course, during the jury selection I would do everything possible to seat jurors with that profile.

Yes, I had a *very good* case, and Daniel Trask himself was making it even better. On top of all that, I drew a federal court judge in Massachusetts who had a history of protecting civil rights and favoring aggrieved parties like ours over big business interests. If I had filed the case in New Hampshire (as the court clerk tried to force me to do), I would have been before a GOP-appointed pro-business judge. So the decision to file in liberal Massachusetts, where the events that led to the claim occurred, was a deliberate part of my strategy. The defendants could not have liked their chances in court even with an army of high-powered attorneys against a make-believe lawyer like me.

Mahoney seemed to reluctantly agree with my analysis on Trask's response and thought that it would be better if Trask refrained from making any more public comments on the matter. "Who approved that response?" I asked. It turned out that Mahoney had not been consulted and that probably some in-house counsel had foolishly done so. Trask sure could have avoided a lot of headaches had someone seen fit to advance me in the competition.

A few days after that conversation with Mahoney, I got an e-mail from Mark Bayliss Productions' business manager, a lawyer whom I'll refer to here as "Robert Starling." Starling stated that he was going to take over the negotiations from Mahoney. I reasoned that they probably didn't want to keep paying Mahoney's high hourly fee and maybe that they blamed him for letting the case spill over into the media when we had ample chance, motive, and opportunity to get it settled quietly before the ninety day RTS period expired. Starling was likely on salary, so there would be no more meters running, generating hourly legal defense bills—at least until court appearances and the trial, which I was sure would be turned over to a litigation team. I doubted that Starling, primarily a business manager, would be entrusted with anything beyond an attempt to settle. Whatever the reason, once Starling took over, things started to go downhill. The whole negotiation process reverted to square one, and all of the progress that Mahoney and I had made evaporated.

The contrast between the former and current attorney couldn't have been greater. Mahoney was the polished patrician professional who specialized in employment law while working for a prestigious law firm under retainer from Daniel Trask. Starling was a younger, fast-talking used car salesman type, in my opinion, working a hybrid job as a business manager/in-house attorney for Mark Bayliss Productions.

While the lawsuit was pending, production of *The Candidate* had ceased, and I was preparing to seek an injunction to keep the show on hiatus until the suit was resolved. During one of our telephone negotiation sessions, I suggested that they could do a celebrity version instead. "If you feature celebrities donating their winnings to charity and no one is actually hired to work for Trask, then you will not be in danger of any EEOC violations," I suggested.

Starling apparently liked the idea, and he later asked me to send him an e-mail granting them permission to produce a celebrity version of the show. I gave them the permission they requested in writing via e-mail.

Before the lawsuit was filed I was close to reaching an amicable settlement agreement with Mahoney, but now we were back to square one, and I was dancing around in circles with attorney Starling. With all progress stalled, Mark Bayliss himself started to get involved in the negotiations on conference calls.

I was very impressed with Bayliss, his honesty and his willingness to cut through the BS and bring the matter to a conclusion. With Bayliss's help and guidance, Starling was free to outline a settlement proposal that was agreeable to me. As the deadline approached to move the matter fully before the federal court, I agreed in principle to what we had discussed via telephone and through our e-mail correspondence. Starling had outside counsel draw up the document and send it to me through registered mail.

When I received the written settlement offer, I was very disappointed to see that it lacked three of the key provisions that Starling had previously promised and agreed to. I sent him an e-mail telling him that I was not happy with the document and that, in my view, he had engaged in an unseemly bait-and-switch tactic. He had clearly promised one thing and delivered another.

Starling responded by telephone with an angry denial that had absolutely no credibility with me because he basically acknowledged that what I said was true, while offering no reasonable defense as to why he left out the key clauses in the document. He lamely offered that he thought that I wasn't interested in those provisions anymore, because I hadn't brought them up again in the most recent conversations. I, of course, had done or said nothing that a reasonable person could infer constituting a release of those sections that we had agreed to. I didn't bring them up again, because those issues had been settled to my satisfaction and Starling had given me his word that he would follow through with his promises. Starling offered to reopen the negotiations to satisfy my concerns.

I was faced with a very tough decision at this point. There was no time to renegotiate the settlement before the impending deadline to make our first court appearance. Proceeding to court involved significant expenses and potential further embarrassment for the defendants because of the number and type of documents that they would be required to file in response to the suit. My own expenses were minimal, as I was personally prosecuting the case on my own without any assistance from "real" lawyers. The court was in Boston, so traveling there wasn't a problem for me.

I eventually decided, out of respect for Daniel Trask, Mark Bayliss, and Mahoney, who had all behaved quite honorably during this process, to sign the settlement with the key clauses missing. My goal from the start was to represent the protected class and gain some measure of notice and relief for them. I had already succeeded in getting more media attention for the issue of age discrimination in the workforce than anyone else had ever done. The settlement, in addition to that, was at least minimally sufficient to call it a day and end the process. At no time did I seek, nor did I gain, monetarily for myself. This wasn't about me, despite what some of the twisted media reports stated. It was *all* about the protected class and my advocacy on their behalf.

. . .

"It's no secret that whenever someone writes or says anything negative about Daniel Trask, or sues him, he almost always responds with a loud, fiery, and sometimes coarse denouncement of that individual. As proof that I earned his respect during this affair, you will note from the public record that Trask never uttered or wrote a single word denouncing me, my character, or my intentions (and I am very thankful to him for that!). That should speak volumes to anyone who chooses to examine or question my account of the events described here. And, of course, if you do doubt my retelling of the events, you could ask Trask and Bayliss themselves. Even a "no comment" would speak volumes.

UNITED STATES DISTRICT COURT

EASTERN DISTRICT OF MASSACHUSETTS

L. RON HOWARD (Pro Se) and others similarly situated, DOES 1-10,000, Plaintiffs, v. TRASK ORGANIZATION INC., a New York Corporation, TRASK PRODUCTIONS, LLC, a New York Corporation, DANIEL TRASK, a New York resident, MARK BAYLISS PRODUCTIONS, INC., a California Corporation, MARK BAYLISS, an Alien residing in the United Kingdom, JOHN WORLDWIDE INC., a California Corporation, ARCHER WORLDWIDE, INC., a California Corporation, AJ WORLDWIDE, INC. a California Corporation, and DOES 1-10, Defendants.	Case No.: 1:07-CV-10007 **COMPLAINT FOR:** **(1) AGE DISCRIMINATION IN HIRING** **REQUEST FOR CLASS-ACTION CERTIFICATION** **DEMAND FOR JURY TRIAL**

Plaintiffs L. Ron Howard and others similarly situated, Does 1-10,000 (collectively "Plaintiffs"), allege as follows:

JURISDICTION

3. This Complaint alleges age discrimination arising under Title VII of the Civil Rights Act (1964) as supplemented by the Age Discrimination in Employment Act (1967) 29 U.S.C. § 621 *et seq.*, as amended. This court has subject matter jurisdiction over these federal questions pursuant to 29 U.S.C. § 626(b) and (c) and 28 U.S.C. § 1331.

4. This Complaint also alleges violations of Massachusetts law arising under the Massachusetts Fair Employment Practices Act, G.L. c. 151B. This court has jurisdiction over these claims pursuant to its supplemental jurisdiction, 29 U.S.C. § 633(a) and (b) and 28 U.S.C. § 13679(a).

VENUE

5. Venue for this action properly lies in this District pursuant to 28 U.S.C. § 1391(a) because a substantial part of the events leading to these claims arose in the District and 1391(d) because one of the named Defendants is an alien. If the claim is certified as a class-action or collective-action, then future named and un-named plaintiffs, currently referred to as "DOES 1-10,000" will be found to reside in most every District in the United States.

SUMMARY OF THE ACTION

6. On January 8, 2004, the first installment of the reality television series known as "The Candidate" aired on the NBJ

television network which broadcast the show to a national audience. The show depicts Mr. Daniel Trask, a defendant in this action ("Trask") in his real-life role as Chairman, President and CEO of The Trask Organization, a real estate and development conglomerate based in New York. The show depicts and centers on Trask as he evaluates a group of job candidates who have applied to become "The Candidate". In weekly installments or episodes, Trask eliminates one or more job candidates from consideration for the position. This continues through the course of a television season or cycle until Trask finally chooses one person as the ultimate winner of The Candidate job. The candidate who is selected to become "The Candidate" is given a one year employment contract at a salary of $250,000. The winner spends the following year as an employee of The Trask Organization or one of Trask's subsidiary or otherwise related corporations. This working relationship sometimes or oftentimes continues beyond the initial one-year contract period.

7. Prior to the airing of the first cycle of The Candidate, approximately 8,000 applicants initially applied for The Candidate job opening. Out of that number, 16 applicants were selected as finalists for The Candidate position. The oldest of the 16 finalists was thirty-six (36) years old.

Prior to Cycle 2, which first aired on September 9, 2004, approximately 40,000 applications were received. Out of that number, 18 applicants were chosen as finalists to become "the next Candidate". The oldest of this group of 18 finalists was thirty-seven (37) years old.

Prior to Cycle 3, which first aired on January 20, 2005, approximately 10,000 applications were received. Out of that number, 18 applicants were chosen as finalists to become "the next Candidate". The oldest of this group of 18 finalists was thirty-nine (39) years old. None of the other 17 finalists were over thirty-nine (39) years old.

Prior to Cycle 4, which first aired on September 22, 2005, approximately 12,500 applications were received. Out of that number, 18 applicants were chosen as finalists to become "the next Candidate". The oldest of this group of 18 finalists was forty-one (41) years old. None of the other 17 finalists were over thirty-nine (39) years old.

Prior to Cycle 5, which first aired on February 27, 2006, approximately 8,000 applications were received. Out of that number, 18 applicants were chosen as finalists to become "the next Candidate". According to 1the "NBJ Official Site" http://www.nbj.com/The_Candidate_5/about.shtml: "Ranging in age from 22–38, these candidates boast degrees from Harvard, Columbia, Northwestern and Cornell University." None of the 18 finalists were over 40 years old.

Prior to Cycle 6, which is scheduled to begin airing on January 07, 2007, an estimated 13,000 applications were received. Out of that number, 18 applicants were chosen as finalists to become "the next Candidate". According to The NBJ official website, none of the 18 finalists is over 39 years old.

Plaintiffs allege that a pattern of age discrimination against the ADEA protected class is clearly in evidence here. Defendants appear to be consistently predisposed to favoring younger job applicants in their selection process. Over the course of six seasons or cycles, approximately 100,000 candidates have applied for these positions. One hundred and six (106) applicants have been selected from this field to become finalists. Only two candidates (out of 106, out of 100,000) who were over 40 years old, were selected to continue with the job interview process featured on the television show. Not even one of the 106 finalists were over

41 years old at the time of their selection. Plaintiffs bring this lawsuit in an effort to halt Defendants from continuing to discriminate against the protected class.

PARTIES TO THE ACTION

8. Plaintiff L. Ron Howard ("Howard"), at all times herein mentioned, is and was an individual residing in the state of New Hampshire. Plaintiff Howard attained standing in this action when he applied for and attended an interview for "The Candidate" in Natick, Massachusetts, on July 9, 2005. Howard was 49 years old at the time of the interview. Howard presented himself as an outstanding candidate who possessed all of the qualities that Trask had previously expressed that he was looking for in his next "Candidate". Trask has commented during the course of his on air interview program that he prized a combination of book smarts and street smarts. Howard's resume reveals that he was a Magna Cum Laude graduate of New Hampshire College with a Bachelor of Science degree in Business Administration. Howard also possess several years of experience maintaining large commercial properties, with particular expertise managing the electrical, HVAC and Information Technology departments. Even though The Trask Organization is primarily in the business of developing, managing and maintaining large commercial properties, most of the finalists who ultimately were selected to compete for these high-level management jobs did not have the type of closely related skills and experience that Howard offered. Regarding so-called street smarts, Howard grew up and prospered on the streets of Lawrence, Massachusetts, a gritty old textile-mill city where the development of street-smart skills are required if one is to survive. Despite having

excellent credentials, as opposed to the vast majority of applicants, Howard was quickly rejected and was not invited to continue on with the selection process. Howard maintains that he was one of a large number of applicants whose candidacy was disregarded or discounted, mostly or partly due to a widespread and prevalent bias against older job applicants that surrounded this hiring process.

9. Plaintiff Howard does not yet know the true names and identities of those Plaintiffs named herein as "others similarly situated" and DOES 1-10,000 and therefore refers to these Plaintiffs by such fictitious names. Howard, or an attorney to be assigned to this case in the future, will amend this complaint, if certified as a class action, to identify many of the real names and identities of these Plaintiffs. Plaintiffs may also amend this complaint, with permission from the court, to include another class or sub-class who were similarly situated and whose civil rights may have been infringed under the Americans With Disabilities Act of 1990.

10. Plaintiff is informed and believes, and therein alleges, that Defendant The Trask Organization ("Trask Org.") is a corporation organized under the laws of the state of New York with its principle place of business in New York, New York. Plaintiff is further informed and believes and on that basis alleges, that Trask Org. is and/or has been engaged in illegal and discriminatory hiring practices via their connection to the reality based television program The Candidate.

11. Plaintiff is informed and believes, and therein alleges, that Defendant Trask Productions, LLC ("Trask Productions") is a corporation organized under the laws of the state of New York with its principle place of business in New York,

New York. Plaintiff is further informed and believes and on that basis alleges, that Trask Productions is and/or has been engaged in illegal and discriminatory hiring practices via their connection to the reality based television program The Candidate.

12. Plaintiff is informed and believes, and therein alleges, that Defendant Daniel Trask ("Trask") is a resident of the state of New York.
Plaintiff is further informed and believes and on that basis alleges, that Trask is and/or has been engaged in illegal and discriminatory hiring practices via his association with the reality based television program The Candidate.

13. Plaintiff is informed and believes, and therein alleges, that Defendant Mark Bayliss Productions is a corporation organized under the laws of the state of California with its principle place of business in Los Angeles, California. Plaintiff is further informed and believes and on that basis alleges, that Mark Bayliss Productions is or has been engaged in illegal and discriminatory hiring practices via their association with the reality based television program The Candidate. Plaintiff is further informed and believes, and therein alleges, that Defendant Mark Bayliss Productions effectively acts or has acted as an employment agency for Defendants The Trask Org., Trask Productions and Trask via their association with the television program The Candidate.

14. Plaintiff is informed and believes, and therein alleges, that Defendant Mark Bayliss is a resident of the United Kingdom. Plaintiff is further informed and believes and on that basis alleges, that Mark Bayliss is or has been engaged in illegal and discriminatory hiring practices via his association with

the reality based television program The Candidate.
Plaintiff is further informed and believes, and therein
alleges, that Defendant Mark Bayliss effectively acts or has
acted as an employment agent or agency for Defendants The
Trask Org., Trask Productions and Trask via his association
with the television program The Candidate.

15. Plaintiff is informed and believes, and therein alleges,
that Defendant John Worldwide Inc., ("John Worldwide")
is a corporation organized under the laws of the state of
California with its principle place of business in Los Angeles,
California. Plaintiff is further informed and believes and
on that basis alleges, that John Worldwide is or has been
engaged in illegal and discriminatory hiring practices via
their association with the reality based television program
The Candidate.
Plaintiff is further informed and believes, and therein
alleges, that Defendant John Worldwide effectively acts or
has acted as an employment agency for Defendants The
Trask Org., Trask Productions and Trask via their association with the television program The Candidate.

16. Plaintiff is informed and believes, and therein alleges, that
Defendant Archer Worldwide Inc., ("Archer Worldwide")
is a corporation organized under the laws of the state of
California with its principle place of business in Los Angeles,
California. Plaintiff is further informed and believes and
on that basis alleges, that Archer Worldwide is or has been
engaged in illegal and discriminatory hiring practices via
their association with the reality based television program
The Candidate. Plaintiff is further informed and believes,
and therein alleges, that Defendant Archer Worldwide
effectively acts or has acted as an employment agency for

Defendants The Trask Org., Trask Productions and Trask via their association with the television program The Candidate.

17. Plaintiff is informed and believes, and therein alleges, that Defendant AJ Worldwide Inc., ("AJ Worldwide") is a corporation organized under the laws of the state of California with its principle place of business in Los Angeles, California. Plaintiff is further informed and believes and on that basis alleges, that AJ Worldwide is or has been engaged in illegal and discriminatory hiring practices via their association with the reality based television program The Candidate. Plaintiff is further informed and believes, and therein alleges, that Defendant AJ Worldwide effectively acts or has acted as an employment agency for Defendants The Trask Org., Trask Productions and Trask via their association with the television program The Candidate.

18. Plaintiffs do not know the true names and capacities of those Defendants sued herein as DOES 1 through 10, inclusive, and therefore sues these Defendants by such fictitious names. Plaintiffs will amend this Complaint to allege their true names and capacities when such are ascertained. Plaintiffs are informed and believe, and on that basis allege, that each of the Defendants sued herein as DOES 1 through 10, inclusive, is in some manner legally responsible for the wrongful acts set forth herein.

19. Plaintiffs are informed and believe, and therein allege, that Defendants, and each of them, are and/or were, at all times herein mentioned, the agents, servants, employees, joint venturers, and/or co-conspirators of each of the other. Defendants, and each of them, at all times herein mentioned, were acting within the course and scope of said

agency, employment, and/or service in furtherance of the joint venture and/or conspiracy.

VENUE

20. Venue is proper in this court pursuant to 28 U.S.C. § 1391(a) and/or (d) because a substantial part of the events giving rise to the claims herein occurred in this District, or, in the alternative, because one or more of the Defendants are aliens.

FACTUAL BACKGROUND AND ALLEGATIONS COMMON TO ALL CLAIMS FOR RELIEF

21. Defendants have been engaged for several years in the design and production of a television program where candidates vie for the prospect of obtaining a real-life job, working as a term, contract employee for a well known person and corporation at a salary of $250,000. Plaintiff Howard applied for said position on July 9, 2005 and was immediately denied. A close empirical inspection of the numbers of people who have made up the applicant pool to date in comparison with the number (and age) of persons who have been selected as finalists for these management positions indicates that a clear and persistent bias is in place that discriminates against persons over 40 years old in the hiring for these "Candidate" positions. Plaintiff Howard filed an age bias complaint with the Equal Employment Opportunity Commission and said Commission issued to him a Right To Sue Notice. Said Right To Sue Notice arrived at Howard's residence via U.S. Postal Service on October 12, 2006, bearing a postmark dated October 10, 2006. Plaintiff Howard maintains that Defendants have no claim to a Bona Fide Occupational Qualification that would exempt them from the hiring

provisions and practices outlined and mandated in the Age Discrimination in Employment Act. Plaintiffs seek damages and penalties in an exact amount to be determined at trial. Plaintiffs also seek reimbursement from Defendants for any and all costs of suit and attorney fees when such fees are allowable by the court.

REQUEST FOR CLASS ACTION CERTIFICATION

22. Plaintiff Howard, on behalf of himself and others similarly situated, hereby request that this lawsuit receive consideration and certification as a Class Action pursuant to F.R.C.P. 23. In the alternative, if Class Action certification is for any reason denied, Plaintiff Howard, on behalf of himself and others similarly situated, do hereby request that this lawsuit receive consideration for certification as a Collective Action under Section 216(b) of the Fair Labor Standards Act (1938) as amended.

PRAYER FOR RELIEF

23. Plaintiff Howard, on behalf of himself and others similarly situated, pray for a judgment against Defendants TRASK ORGANIZATION INC., TRASK PRODUCTIONS, LLC, DANIEL TRASK, MARK BAYLISS PRODUCTIONS, INC., MARK BAYLISS, JOHN WORLDWIDE, INC., ARCHER WORLDWIDE, INC., AJ WORLDWIDE, INC., and DOES 1-10 for violations of the Age Discrimination in Employment Act in association with their activities in selecting job candidates for a televised program known as "The Candidate" as outlined above in paragraphs 1 through 20.
Plaintiffs seek damages and penalties in an exact amount to be determined at trial. Plaintiffs also seek judgment for

reimbursement from Defendants for any and all costs of suit and attorney fees when such fees and reimbursements are allowable by the court.

24. Plaintiffs seek an injunction ordering the Defendants to cease to engage in the discriminatory practices herein outlined in paragraphs 1 through 21.

CLAIM FOR RELIEF

25. For Plaintiffs and against all Defendants, this lawsuit seeks a claim for relief on the charge of age discrimination.

26. For attorney's fees and costs of suit as provided by statute or otherwise; and

27. For exemplary and punitive damages as provided by statute or otherwise; and

28. For such other and further relief as the Court deems just, equitable, and proper.

DATED: January 4, 2007   By: *L. Ron Howard*
                                             L. Ron Howard
                                             Plaintiff

DEMAND FOR JURY TRIAL

Plaintiff hereby requests a trial by jury.

DATED: January 4, 2007   By: *L. Ron Howard*
                                             L. Ron Howard
                                             Plaintiff

2015

Aspirations

In March, Daniel Trask formed a presidential exploratory committee and made a swing through New Hampshire. Ron hired on as a consultant for a rival campaign (SamSpike.com).

Trask officially announced his candidacy for President of the United States on June 16.

. . .

This concludes the sneak peek into future volumes of *Journey* and *SecretAgentMan*.

Volume 2 will be released only if Volume 1 sells over one hundred thousand copies worldwide. So if you enjoy the story and would like to see it continue, please consider telling your friends and posting links to SecretAgentMan.org on your social media accounts.

Kind regards,
Richard Saunders

ACKNOWLEDGMENTS

I am forever grateful to my supporters who preordered this book before it was published. Without all of you, I would never have met the crowdfunding level that was required. You helped prove that this novel was capable of building a market that was large enough to justify winning a publishing contract. Unfortunately, there is not enough room to list all of you individually here. The full list of supporters can be found on my website SecretAgentMan.org.

James McNamara, Brian Zola, Ed Sabbagh, Dane Morruzzi, Gary Trenholm, Clyde Daly, James Doherty, Michael Osmont, Kevin Murphy, Russell J. Tomassian, William Smith, Cheryl White, Eric Sit, and Geoffrey Bernstein.

Stephen Hewett, Heather Rastello, John M. Kelley, Jim Keenan, Dolores M Hewett, Helen Morris, Trung Nguyen, Gwen Owen, Kevin B. Roche, Frederick S. Powers, Joshua M. Weiss, Russell Haloon, Peter A. Hewett, Jr., Steven M. Flynn, Nicholas Bouzianis, Brian J. Smith, Kerrie Ganley, Richard Manganaro, Donna Mitchell, Tyrone E. Rachel, Ann Lozier, Teresa S. Klingenstein, Fred Goforth, Greg Flamand, Greg Pacheco, Chris Sylvester, Rick Alluzio, Adam Rooney, Tony Graceffa, Tom O'Neill, Steve Bransfield, Elizabeth A. Moruzzi, Velvet Hewett, Nathaniel Crosby, Amanda Lankford, Joshua Taube, Reader Writer, Brett Brusky, and Esben Ringgaard.

INKSHARES

Inkshares is a crowdfunded book publisher. We democratize publishing by having readers select the books we publish—we edit, design, print, distribute, and market any book that meets a pre-order threshold.

Interested in making a book idea come to life? Visit inkshares.com to find new book projects or to start your own.

ABOUT THE AUTHORS

Mykl Walsh and Richard Saunders consider themselves to be "citizens of the world." Mr. Walsh wishes to remain anonymous. Saunders is currently managing director of ThePhoenixFoundation.net.